WHAT THE
KNOCKER-UPPER
WOKE UP

SARAH J MAXWELL

WHISPER PUBLISHING

WHISPER PUBLISHING
www.whisperpublishing.co.uk
info@whisperpublishing.co.uk

1st Edition

Paperback ISBN: 978-1-7395943-2-9
eBook ISBN: 978-1-7395943-3-6

To my fantastic son, 'picker-upper' and bringer of joy and laughter. And to my fabulous husband, 'fixer-upper' and love of my life.

ACKNOWLEDGEMENTS

So many people to thank, but first up, my incredible publisher, Whisper. Wendy, you've been a tower of strength, despite the struggles of the past year. You are an inspiring woman, and I'm grateful for all you've done for me. Mark, quietly in the background, doing his thing. Never disappoints. Thank you. Huge thanks also to Anna, my fabulous agent at Intersaga. A breath of fresh air, and another strong, inspiring woman. Always fighting my corner. You're the best!

Simon, Liz, and Will, what would I do without you? Cheering me on. Supporting me. Building me up when I doubted. I love you more than you know, and grateful for your enduring belief.

To my Australian family. Your encouragement and love mean the world.

Thank you to every fabulous friend I've made on social media. Those that buy my books, read, and review. More than that, support and encourage.

Thanks to my real-life friends. Those I've known for forty years and longer. Those I met on stage. Those I rarely see. Those who've only recently claimed a friend spot. Not sure what I'd do without you guys. Thank you for always being there. And thanks to my brothers and their beautiful families. You guys are awesome, and I love you with everything.

To every beta/arc reader, please know, I greatly appreciate your time and effort and highly value your comments.

And, of course, to you, the reader. Thanks for taking a chance on my book.

If you enjoy *What the Knocker-Upper Woke Up*, the author would appreciate a quick review on Amazon, Goodreads, or your favourite book website. Reviews are vital. A few words matter.

GLOSSARY

Baba Jaga (Baba Yaga)

In Slavic folklore, *Baba Jaga* (from Polish), is a supernatural ogress who steals, cooks, and eats her victims, usually children. Though appearing as deformed and ferocious, she is more of a trickster encouraging transformation.

Horologist

A person skilled in the practice or theory of horology. A maker of clocks or watches.

Horology

The study and measurement of time.

Knocker-Upper (knocker-up)

A human alarm clock working ungodly hours, who roused workers to work using long sticks, rattles, soft hammers, or pea-shooters.

Before and during Britain's Industrial Revolution, watches and mechanical alarm clocks were rare, expensive, and unreliable. Being a knocker-upper was a respected profession. The practice spread rapidly across the country, mainly in mill towns, in areas of poorly paid shift workers, or in London, where dockers kept strange hours depending on the tides.

Knocking up was so common in London, Charles Dickens referenced it in his classic novel, *Great Expectations.*

WHAT THE
KNOCKER-UPPER
WOKE UP

PART I

Old London

1

The Asylum

Martin Turner was not a boy worth remembering, so when he went missing, no one did. Apart from his mother, and memories of her eldest son, blurred by a mother's tears, contrived a much nicer boy than he'd ever been.

He was there the night the asylum burned down. Saw it from the corner of his eye as he loped along, hoping to find something worth stealing. Martin often lurked near the Old Gin Palace. Drunks were easy targets, but that night, he was distracted.

Orange flames leapt high, the white moon making fiery arms shimmer. Devoid of common sense, Martin watched, a foolish grin on his pale, spotty face. He sensed his luck was about to change. The flames grew higher, brighter, silver swords spearing the sky, while sparks of golden sovereigns showered from above, as if from heaven.

Beneath the burning building, roots spread sideways, carrying the stench of death and a memory of greed, but to foolish eyes, the roots glittered and glowed. Warm. Full of promise and hope. Martin was unaware the roots were underfoot, feeling his life, absorbing his energy. The longer he stood, desiring what was false, the more life those roots took until there was almost nothing left. Until he was a grey husk, ready to crumble to dust.

Martin Turner was never seen again, trapped as he was within the grey shroud of Sideways.

One week later, exalted from his endeavours abroad, Able Seaman Carter visited the Old Gin Palace to celebrate his safe return to England. Full of wine and high spirits, he collected a street girl and, for unfathomable reasons, took her to the site of the old asylum. After completing the transaction, Carter caught a carriage home, where he took to his bed, staying put for a considerable length of time.

He left his bed a different man, with a sallow complexion and pale eyes, wincing at every noise, trembling at shadows. Sideways had slid inside his soul and changed him. Ever after, every decision he made, or never made, led to a life plagued with unhappiness.

The street girl wasn't so lucky. Annie Franklin fell asleep in that strange, desolate place, and it would be many years before she turned to dust. Even then, her destiny was to drift alone, an insignificant speck.

Sideways was forever and, in a gloomy corner of thickest shadow, something stirred.

2

Smelly Mary

The smell was wrong. A rotting cesspit of wrong. A fetid juggernaut of smell hitting Mary head on, prickling with intent inside her nostrils. The stink made its way to the back of her throat and stung her eyes.

Mary was good at ignoring things. She could ignore her impetigo and interminable hunger. Even fleas feasting on her flesh, and brutal decay eroding her teeth. But not the smell creeping towards her. She couldn't ignore that. She stood Sideways in front of the scorched building, hearing screams and wails that once echoed around the stone prison. Grey walls smeared in blood, scarred by the scratches of hundreds of fingernails.

The place was once a mental asylum. Mary's mother had lived and died there, then it burned down. Perhaps some orderly, desperate to escape the torment and torture of the inmates, had taken a candle to it. No one survived the fiery tsunami that engulfed the kitchen and roared towards the sky. Outlined against a smoggy skyline, the ruined building was the only memorial to those poor souls. Broken, blackened, yet resolute. All but erased from people's memories and the bleak landscape camouflaged against Victorian London's sombre sky.

Those living near the remains of the institution, not quite Sideways, were unfortunate creatures who lived in the Old Quarter. Close to four hundred people, often a dozen or more to each tiny, two-roomed dwelling. These *quarter-siders* had more than their share of rats and fleas, and well-to-do *outsiders* believed the Great Stink of 1858 wouldn't have been as deadly if the fire that consumed the institution had consumed the Old Quarter as well.

Now, something bigger than the Great Stink was coming.

What was it Mary could smell and no one else could? Poverty and gin kept minds dull. No one noticed drunken marauders who went missing, or street girls disappearing, and no one talked about mothers who called in vain for children who never came. If they did, they were drained of colour, as if somewhere they'd left their soul.

Spending her days stalking the streets, Mary was a vagrant, vigorously avoided and considered a stinking pile of flea-infested filth. Indeed, that was the case. Her armpits were bags of putrid meat, her breath reeked of rotting garbage, and weeping sores stank of open sewers. During the Great Stink, not long after the institution was lost, when Mary was older than fifteen, but younger than fifty—impossible to tell under the rags and coats of dirt—she felt quite at home.

Mary used her nose to see, for despite her general ignorance, she knew better than to believe everything she saw with her eyes. She listened too. Heard whispered warnings trickling through the sewers of cobbled streets. London streets fervently avoided. Dark, even in daylight, where shadows lurked in corners and waited. Mary smelled the rats' fear as they scurried to outrun the thing that was coming.

Sideways wasn't somewhere that should exist. It wasn't of heaven or earth and, if Mary had been a learned scholar a century ahead of her time, she would have likened it to a black hole. All she knew was her world was in trouble and she felt the burden of responsibility.

Hunched within her rags and haggard in her body, she saw the building for what it was. An incubator for a monster. Stewing in smouldering embers, born from chaos within troubled walls and far more distracting than Mary's open sores and scores of fleas.

She sat down amid the swirling grey and closed her eyes, sensing the smell rising from the ground, exploring her, trying to drain her colour. She felt the truth of who she was igniting within, surety scorching tentacles of stink from her body. Saw how the smell hid. How Sideways could appear silver or gold, or brimful of promise and warmth. Mary smelt danger. Protectively, she wrapped her own smell around her. She had no business with Sideways. Not that day.

She opened her eyes and gazed towards her city, her London, and glimpsed a terrible future. Beloved streets engulfed by Sideways. "Not on my watch," she hissed through embers of teeth.

Hobbling back to the Old Quarter, Mary paid her last penny for a gin and contemplated life. Hers was simple, and for that she was grateful, but she had to warn the populace about Sideways, about the slumbering creature that would one day come. A creature made up of despair and madness. A creature who absorbed the anguish of every inmate. Embracing the cruel greed of the dead Matron, a fleshy woman who wore a cudgel like a cross and snatched at shiny pennies.

On bunioned feet, Mary trailed across the city streets, giving voice to her fears. "You can see it if you really try, from the corner of your eye." She stopped gentlemen attempting to cross the road to avoid her stench, and halted ladies who recoiled from filthy, grabbing fingers. "It lures the traveller, weak of mind …"

Traps the greedy, hoping to find.
Entices the child who wants to play,

ensnaring the night and keeping the day.

Mary moved from pub to pub and sat at sticky tables. Eyes full of terrible wisdom, she breathed a warning that stank of the Great Stink. "Sideways creeps and crawls and waits. Run away from its hellish gates."

People ignored or laughed at her, but she had stood at those hellish gates and knew someday someone would wake something up. She was as certain of that as she was of the family of mice living within the folds of her rags.

And soon she wakes, and she will take.
So, do not stop, and do not see,
the Sideways Lady comes for me.

Mary had the longevity of something preserved. In fact, she was partially pickled in gin, but it wasn't just that. She was an intrinsic part of London Town. Its flesh and bones. The perfectly preserved heart beating inside her chest was the heart of London. This was how Mary defied age. She was the steadfast buildings looming over the city streets or foul-smelling Old Father Thames snaking endlessly towards the sea.

Mary knew she had a long journey ahead, but for now, she waited. The monster waited, too. Patient. Watchful. The soul of the Matron flourishing within its new host. Putrefying the air. Plotting.

In that fashion, fifty years passed by, until the Knocker-Upper came knocking.

3

The Knocker-Upper

Despite the dull moon casting its gloomy prospect upon murky streets, the pavement shone as though stitched together with silver thread. Surrounded by stone and an acrid stink, Alice might have been at the bottom of a dark, dismal well, but magic glimmered beneath her feet.

With scuffed, ill-fitting shoes and a thrill of excitement, Alice stepped upon silver strands. Intrepid. Certain the street shone only for her and trusted her with a sovereign secret. Following the trail invigorated Alice. She imagined the silver working its way through the holes of her shoes, into her feet, up skinny legs. Warming her as she traversed grim, narrow streets.

She passed an old, blind dog. The creature barked, startling her, and for a moment, Alice forgot why she was there. She stared into the dog's milky eyes. He stared back, heaving a frail frame upright, wobbling on spindly legs. He barked again, his tail wafting back and forth, seeming to smile at her, or maybe trying to remind her of something. Exhausted, the animal slumped to the ground and Alice remembered. The trail would have to wait. She was a Knocker-Upper and had a job to do.

Clutching her pea-shooter, Alice skipped towards Attic Row. At number three, she peered up at the dark bedroom window where Mr Wattle slept with Mrs Wattle and two children. She put the pea-shooter to her mouth, aimed, and fired. A shrivelled, grey pea chinked against the window. Alice counted to ten, then made to blow a second pea, when a disembodied hand affected a sleepy wave. Humming, she skipped away.

Before the sun was up, Alice had woken Mr Wattle, Mr Roper, Mrs Chance, Mr Fisher, and Mr Moody. She also woke Mrs Herring, who needed five peas!

She still had to rouse Mr Smith, the clock man, who lived alone since his wife died and his son went off to school. Quite well-to-do, Mr Smith was the sole proprietor of Smith & Son, the clock shop. A gentleman, devoid of extravagance and self-indulgence, Smith was a quiet sort of fellow who preferred his own company to that of any other.

The stiff gentleman once said to Alice, in the low rumble that was his voice: "You, my dear, are no bother, with your little flying missiles landing against my window at five am. Unlike the maid knocking on my door, who demands much more attention, such as 'morning,' or 'fetch my tea,' and I would rather not spend my morning in idle chit-chat."

Alice had giggled because it seemed a funny thing for the gentleman to say when he seemed to enjoy talking so much. She liked Mr Smith and didn't care how much he talked, or didn't talk, since he always paid her a penny that was shiny and new.

Like every morning before, Alice wandered the dirty streets in her beloved red coat, which was growing far too small but, unlike other mornings, Alice wandered into the Old Quarter. There was no one to wake there, but Alice was following the silver trail. The sun replaced the moon, so it was no longer dark, but swirly and grey. The only sound was the noise her feet made against the stone. Like muffled footsteps. Alice felt small, insignificant, and the usually peaceful silence grew restless. If she'd faltered, she would've known that silence shouldn't be restless, and the sky had no business being draped so low.

Alice walked fast. She didn't like the smell of the Old Quarter. A mixture of urine and gin and rotting vegetables. It was a terrible smell, but never as bad as the Great Stink that Granny Edith once described as the 'devil's stinking pot of putrid stew.' She told Alice it hovered over London like poison, killing people with its toxic fumes.

Alice knew the smell of the Old Quarter wouldn't kill her, but she didn't like it there. Didn't like its stillness, how it echoed, as though everything was buried under blankets of quiet. She followed the silver and tried not to think about the bad things Granny Edith told her.

Muttering from a toothless mouth, the old woman warned. "There's only ever forwards or backwards, Alice. Never go Sideways because that will make you a Sideways Person, and you might never find your way home."

Alice loved her mama, sister, and two brothers, even her dad—whom she rarely saw—but she hated the fleas and her dirty skin. She dreamed of being an outsider one day, or better, going somewhere far from London, where beasts called cows lived in fields and ate grass. She became a Knocker-Upper to earn money for food. She liked clutching gleaming pennies in her hand and dreaming of fine dresses and shiny curls.

That morning, those things seemed more possible than they'd ever been, and were all that mattered. She hummed as she walked, silver glinting from the corner of her eye. Magic. Impossible to resist. She didn't realise she was walking Sideways until it was too late. Too late to knock up Mr Smith, who, on waking, would know the morning was different. Would feel it in the ominous ticking of his clocks.

Alice didn't smell the smell waiting to hold her, couldn't hear the frantic heartbeat of London as she left her path. She saw only the glint of silver and felt warm inside. The Old Quarter was behind her, and before her—though actually Sideways—was the asylum, burned down many years before and never rebuilt. Alice gazed at the building. Jagged against a brooding sky, it reminded her of rotten teeth. Tarnished stone. Crumbled. Misshapen. Beautiful in a way and Alice, who'd never owned paper and pens, imagined how it would look if someone could draw it. Terrible, yet magnificent.

Despite the prickle at her dirty neck, Alice believed she was where she was meant to be. She edged closer to the ruined institution, unaware her feet ever moved. Spellbound, she wished when the building burned it had burned to nothing, but there it stood, half alive. Or half dead. Rows of splintered windows stared mournfully. Glazed eyes with frayed rags, hanging like frozen tears.

Alice loaded a grey missile into her pea-shooter and gawped at one bigger, unbroken, window. The window stared back. She shot the pea, but the window remained unblinking. She crept closer and shot again, but the window mocked. Alice stumbled nearer, crunching over the crumbling bones of the building. With two blue eyes, she stared into the doleful, fixed eye, shot a third missile, and watched the pea land in its centre. Behind the dark eye, rags moved.

Alice was a Knocker-Upper, but it didn't occur to her she might be waking something up. As blue eyes stared into the black eye, Alice knew, too late, she was Sideways People now.

4

Bone, Sand, and Ice

Dread. Squirming around in Alice's tummy. Uncoiling, filling her up so there wasn't much left of her. In those passing seconds, in the time it would take Mr Smith, the clock man, to notice Alice, the Knocker-Upper was unusually late, her fate was sealed.

Alice saw movement behind the window, then a terrible smell slammed into her. A stench worse than the Old Quarter. More noxious even than the Great Stink. Alice guessed it was the thing that moved. The thing waking up. The thing *she* had woken up.

She should have run home. Having just woken, the creature would be slow, unsure of itself and its capabilities. Alice would have seen Mama again. She may have always had a fragment of Sideways inside, but destiny is kind to some people, and would have been kind to Alice.

Her relationship with Mr Smith flourished. Under his guidance, she learned how to read and when Charles came home from school, the young Alice fell in love. Devastated when he left for the Great War, she kept reading, and developed a passion for the intricacies of a clock. *Deft little fingers that could take apart a timepiece and reassemble as Mr Smith watched on, delighted with his protégée. The little clock shop felt like home. The smell of dust and oil, comforting. The creak of floorboards, reassuring. Most of all, the sound of ticking assuaged the torment in her mind, keeping Sideways at bay.*

When Charles Smith arrived home from the war, minus one leg, he needed constant care. Upon discharge from a fine London hospital, Mr Smith thought to employ the services of Alice to care for his son. After all, he could see Charles was smitten with the young lady. In time, Mr Smith happily bestowed a generous fortune upon the couple, which meant escape from London to the country. To a cottage with views of wild countryside splattered with black and white cows.

Alice sometimes dreamed of Sideways, and on occasion, the grey inside frightened her. But London was far away, and she lived a happy life with Charles and their three children, dying on her 67th birthday, a day after her beloved husband.

None of those things would happen because Alice didn't run home. Instead, she hid behind piles of scorched rubble and tried to pretend the thing moving down the crumbling stairs wasn't real. It was no use. She knew the rhyme Granny Edith taught her. *She'd woken the Sideways Lady.* Through gaps in the wall, she spied a monstrous creation, shrouded by a cloak made from Sideways, with agitated patterns of grey and billowing folds like washing on a windy day.

With her pungent smell, the creature lifted her head and sniffed. Poor Alice made herself as small as possible, shifting rubble underfoot, then she heard a noise that reminded her of laundry day. A big copper pot and in the pot, a stew of boiling sheets. Under Mama's watchful eye and balancing upon a stool, Alice wielded the wooden laundry stick, plunging the soiled garments beneath the scummy surface. The stew gurgled and frothed with every plunge, slurping, sucking, gushing water from sodden bed sheets.

The Sideways Lady gurgled and slurped as she laughed.

Alice screwed her eyes shut. Despite the horror of burbling merriment, something strange happened. She saw herself crouching behind the ruined building. A tiny red speck, trapped and afraid, but what did it matter if there was a braver Alice, one that could see and not be seen? Filled with horror, but invisible, Alice the Brave gazed upon the Sideways Lady and saw what she was. A gruesome imitation of a woman, but bigger than any she'd ever seen. Even bigger than any man she'd seen. Stooped and wide. A slab of stone with giant hands dangling loose and shining fingers like uncooked sausages. Beneath the ripples of grey cloak, Alice glimpsed an eerie sheen of pasty flesh.

With a last glance at the motionless shape of her other self, Alice the Brave fled. She tore through Sideways, blind at first, catching sight of the sun glinting on a window. No longer certain she wasn't dreaming, she focused on the light's glare, trying to ignore the odd sensation of still feeling invisible. Soundless and see through. Surely, Mama would make it all right, once wrapped in her wide embrace. Snuggled deep, inhaling her smell.

The old dog barked as Alice hurtled by, but her feet no longer echoed along the cobbled stones of the Old Quarter, now alive with noise and filling up with the stench of sweating bodies. Indoors, Alice fell sobbing to the ground. Her tears went unheard, her crumpled frame unseen, because she was still huddled beside the old asylum and the Sideways Lady was wondering whether to eat the small red child or keep her as a pet.

Oblivious to her daughter's plight, Alice's mama went about her usual routine. Vigorous scrubbing of the front step followed by arduous mending of torn, worn clothes. Only when she heard the clatter and clamour of the shrimp cart and the bellow of the sherbet seller from a distant corner, did she wonder why Alice hadn't returned home from knocking-up. She didn't worry. Her daughter possessed a fancy for daydreaming that wreaked havoc with routine.

Golden streaks gleamed through heavy smog as another London morning broke. It would be the last morning Alice saw. Dad and older brother Tommy were already at work and sister Mollie helped with Samuel, no longer a chubby baby, more a troubled old man who knew crying wouldn't quell the hole of hunger in his belly. With no more tears left inside, Alice watched Mollie struggle with Samuel's socks. He offered no resistance, but the socks were old and shrunken from the continual boiling they'd endured since Tommy was an infant.

Babies may not be able to speak, but the world's prejudices haven't diluted their minds, so they may see or understand things in a way the more informed individual cannot. Quietly, Samuel lay contemplative, noticing a shimmer next to Mollie. A blurred nothing shape. Samuel knew the blur was his other sister, the one who sang softly to him and held him until he went to sleep. He snuffled and cooed, but his shimmering sister made no reply. Kicking his leg, the sock Mollie had tugged half on flew off and landed in a dark corner.

Mollie remonstrated. A seven-year-old trying to sound like her mama. "Bad baby. Bad Samuel. And now the sock will be dirty."

Alice stumbled into the family bedroom and crumpled upon the thin mattress.

Mama called out to Mollie. "I'm going to look for Alice. Take care of your brother."

The gentle voice left Alice riddled with pain. She curled up in a ball trying to ease it, but the pain didn't lessen, and Alice noticed, for the first time in a long time, the absence of the scratch of fleas. Small consolation. She listened to sounds outside in the street, her baby brother's cry, and her sister's attempts at consoling him.

"Sing to him, Mollie," she whispered, drifting among sheets smelling mildly of sweat, wondering if she was lost forever. That was too terrible to contemplate, so Alice closed her eyes and willed herself to sleep, because Mama decreed sleep to be the fixer of things.

Alice woke in the stinking void of Sideways and could still feel the coarse bedsheet upon her flesh. Still hear Mollie's persistent chatter and Samuel's cry, but all faded to nothing. She was alone and afraid. Rubble stirred as she moved, cold, numb, but no longer invisible. She waggled her fingers, felt the painful pummelling of her heart. A bird inside the cage of her chest.

Had it all been a terrible dream? One that came with you when you woke up. Alice tried to shrug it off, to believe everything was as it should be, but like maggots in a rotten apple, something inside told her no. The Great Stink, she recalled, was the devil's pot of putrid stew. Perhaps Sideways was the leftovers. And the Sideways Lady? Perhaps *she* was the devil cloaked with the devil's stink. A rotting corpse in an open grave stink.

Dark and foreboding, the asylum loomed. Alice sniffed the air, certain *she* wasn't there, but how had she not recoiled from the stench when she first stumbled Sideways? Of course! She'd been lured. The stink had always been there, hiding inside the silver path she'd followed. Now, she saw nothing through the immense, grey blanket. Sideways enveloped her, touching her flesh. Shuddering, she imagined the probing tentacles of a giant sea creature and whimpered.

Fearful of the vast ocean, Alice shuffled towards the asylum and ascended the rickety stairs. Inside, she saw the remains of a large entrance hall. In one corner, a narrow flight of stone steps led down, but Alice didn't like the dark shadow. A blot of ink slowly spreading towards her.

Stemming fear, she climbed a larger, broken staircase, then scrambled higher with no thought to falling.

At the top, Alice turned left, making footprints in the soot, thinking of the shadow downstairs. *Had it touched her? Was she a shadow, too?* Footprints morphed into ghoulish shapes watching her. Alice licked bone dry lips. A vast, gloomy room yawned before her. Once a dormitory, Alice supposed, the beds were now cruel metal monsters, black and twisted in macabre fashion. She tiptoed towards a tiny, barred window and noticed a bed that had defied time and the fire. The thin mattress covered in blankets the colour of nothing, corners crisp from flames. Nestled among the blankets was a doll. Alice stared in horror. Part of its face had caved, and one blue eye peered out.

Recoiling, Alice retreated from the room and headed to the end of the hallway and another room. One window, without bars, a forlorn black rag hanging. Alice didn't like the feel of the room. An unseen evil presence lurking. She made to back away, but something out in the vastness of Sideways caught her eye. Ignoring the fear gnawing at her insides, she walked to the window, peered out, and spied a house. Though it was far away, it seemed near, as though seen through the magic eye glass the clock man used. The one he'd once let her look through. At the front door of the house, she saw her mother crying and wringing her hands together.

"Mama," Alice choked.

Someone else replied. "Come out. Come out. Wherever you are."

Alice had been cold before, but the Sideways Lady's voice split her soul, leaving splinters of ice. She knew she'd never grow old. That she was a speck of dust. A broken doll. Or worse, a pet.

Sideways was home. Forever.

5

The Smell of Fear

The morning was chilly. An unnatural bite to a summer's day. Standing outside his clock shop, Mr Smith, the horologist, shivered. He loitered for some time, listening to the sound of London waking up.

The street where his clock shop stood was tucked away, peaceful among the chaos of the nearby meat market and London Bridge, but that morning Mr Smith found the emptiness unnerving. Instinct told him something was wrong, and it was no surprise when a policeman strolled towards him.

"I understand you use the services of a knocker-upper? A young lady called Alice?" The constable glanced at the clock shop, his confusion clear.

"She didn't arrive this morning—"

"Her mother reported her missing."

Earlier that fateful morning, when the sky appeared brushed with inky streaks, Mr Smith awoke with a prickle of unease. Drawn towards a dingy back room, he scanned the murky depths behind his shop, squinting into the Sideways gloom, seeing something but nothing. Unease kept Mr Smith awake, before exhaustion stole over him and he fell asleep where he sat. Subsequently, he was late opening his shop.

The news of Alice's disappearance spread, and Mr Smith received the sympathies of his neighbours since they all knew he used her services. The irony of him being a horologist, a local *expert* on time, wasn't lost on any of them. Mr Smith tinkered with clock parts and thought about the missing child. *A happy little sparrow.* She was polite and articulate, despite being born close to the Old Quarter.

He didn't dare mention Sideways to the police officer, since it was something rarely alluded to and often not believed, but Mr Smith knew better, and couldn't help wondering at the burst of red he'd seen in the early hours. A glimpse of colour before being swallowed inside the grey. One second there, the next gone. *Something, but nothing.*

His mother told him about Sideways when he was young, and he had no reason to doubt her, even when he was old enough to understand his mother was considered eccentric. She'd once been an actress, flamboyant in dress, and had refused to hand over her only child entirely to a nanny. His father, twelve years his wife's senior, and smitten from the day he'd seen her playing Lady Macbeth on a London stage, allowed her the freedom that ensured her happiness. But the surging stink always troubled Mrs Smith, and she warned her son to stay away. He mostly complied.

With Sideways lapping at the locked and bolted back door, years passed and renowned horologist, Mr Smith—married, a father, widowed—allowed himself the luxury of believing he might die without experiencing another incident. Then Alice went missing and left the man besieged with guilt.

In the shadows of that evening, Smith stepped outside his shop. The noise of the day—muted, constant yelling from the meat market—had quieted, replaced soon by the chaotic night. Drunken lollygagging and laughter that would lead to raucous singing. Mr Smith listened and watched as someone appeared from nowhere. He'd known of Smelly Mary since childhood. When alive, his mother possessed a distasteful desire to seek out the old woman and converse with her. Hushed whispers that intrigued the little boy, but never enough for him to get too close since the woman's aroma repelled him.

Smelly Mary was old, or so Mr Smith presumed, and probably more than a little mad. He couldn't remember a time when she wasn't *there.* As a boy, he recalled seeing her looking much the same as she did now. Old, but not old, and always hobbling with intent, as if she had something of the utmost importance to impart.

"Before you repose for the evening, have you seen 'er?" Although Mary's coarse London dialect could jar and the letter aitch might disappear altogether, the woman possessed a surprising vocabulary.

"No, Madam, I have not. Have you?" Mr Smith searched his pocket for a penny. His fingers clasped the coin.

Mary snatched without thanks. "She won't be coming back, not like she was before. Not since she waked *her* up."

"Who has she woken up?" Sweat prickled across Mr Smith's forehead. He didn't think he'd like where this conversation was going.

Mary drew closer, blinking fierce eyes. "I always knew she'd be waked up one day. I smelled it a long time ago. *The nose knows.* All these years, I've been watching and waiting, and telling folk about Sideways, 'oping the day wouldn't come, but it came anyways."

Wringing filthy hands, Smelly Mary shook her head in a sombre fashion. Mr Smith tried to step back, but the closed door of the shop stood steadfastly behind him. He trembled, trapped beneath a steely gaze. "What do you mean?"

"You know. I can see it in your eyes, and I saw it in your mother's eyes, too. *She's* out there. Wandering. Large as life and with a soul as black as the devil's. She'll be unstoppable, and Sideways'll spread its poison over the land."

Mr Smith nodded. Smelly Mary made perfect sense on the stoop of his shop, though later he'd question his own sanity because, of course, the reality was much harder to digest than hearsay.

"Much money you got?" Mary asked.

Mr Smith recoiled, fumbling in his pocket again, trying not to think about the sensation of the lady's bosom against his chest. "What do you need?"

She jerked her head towards his shop. "Not for me. That land out there. You need to acquire it."

"Madam, what possible reason is there to buy?"

Mary gripped Mr Smith's arm, claws clutching their prey. "I imagine you read plenty, so picture this. A merciless creature, invisible beneath a vast sea, and hungry. Prey is lured t'wards it, then it rises up and snatches you down. That's what Sideways is, the sea and the creature, that's *her*."

"Yes, but what am I to do?"

Mary ignored Mr Smith's dismay. She needed him to feel afraid. Fear might be the only weapon. That and a parlour trick of magic fire. "For now, the sea's penned, held back by an invisible barrier. Your shop, the Old Gin Palace, and the blacksmiths must never be destroyed, or London will be lost."

"What do you mean?" Mr Smith spluttered, his face glowing red.

Mary looked at him as though he were stupid and somehow, faced with the filthy, illiterate vagrant in front of him, Mr Smith *felt* stupid.

She puffed out a sigh, breathing her foul-smelling breath across the poor man's face. "If the barriers aren't in place, the sea will spill out."

"I see." Mr Smith licked dry lips, fumbling with a tight collar that fitted perfectly before. In the evening chill, he saw Smelly Mary's wisdom. Could smell her fear, too. His mother had been right to trust this woman. Her stink, the dirt, even the fleas, meant nothing. He would buy the land and, if necessary, provide a light for lost souls.

"The Sideways Lady is awake, and she's rotten inside. Greedy too. Mark my words, she won't think twice about taking what's not 'ers. She'll devour every poor soul that gets lost, 'til one day, God willing, someone'll make 'er go back to sleep."

"*H—how* is she to be made to go back to sleep?"

Mary screwed up her face until it looked like a prune. Watering eyes blinked rapidly. "No idea."

"Then what …"

Mary placed a bony finger upon Smith's breastbone, cutting him off. "You better 'ope that one day, someone'll understand and send her back to the grave. In the meantime, my best advice to you is, never forget."

"What will you do?" Mr Smith rasped.

"I liked that girl. Knew 'er grandmother, Edith. *I must do something.*" Mary glanced along the empty street, first one way, then the other, then fixed the hapless man with a glower. "I'm going out there to find 'er and look after 'er best I can."

"I think I saw her. At least there was something red in all that terrible grey. Just for a moment."

Smelly Mary's eyes sparkled in the gloom. "She wears that little red coat. Show me."

Mr Smith didn't sleep well that night. Finally, when the sky was still an inkblot, he pushed back his bedclothes, donned slippers, and dressing gown, and crept to the back window. He looked beyond his courtyard into the realm of Sideways. Scoured the expanse of dead land. He was afraid of it, had always been afraid. As a boy, he had the small back room, but rarely opened the window for fear of letting in the smell. Nightmares came anyway, shadows moving like sludge to gobble him up. His mother was passionate, whispering advice to ward off danger.

'Be yourself, Thomas. Know who you are, *like* who you are and then, if you ever find yourself Sideways, you'll be able to march right out again.' Her green eyes flashed in warning. 'Whatever you do, if you're stuck there, don't close your eyes and don't go to sleep.'

Only once did Mr Smith venture as far as the old asylum. He tried to warn his friend Tom Finch, but the boy was already ensnared, certain he spied treasure within the undulating grey. When Tom eventually stumbled from Sideways, he was changed. Confused. Eyes faded. The way wet paint dries and fades. Tom Finch had Sideways inside and for the rest of his insignificant life, never made a single good decision, but plenty of bad ones.

Mr Smith shivered, climbed back into bed, and stayed awake until it was time to get up again. During those waking hours, he vowed the first thing he would do at the start of the new day was contact Mr Barlow, the lawyer, and ask about buying the land behind his shop. He felt momentarily relieved. Then, as dawn broke over number 4 Barricade Street, he found himself delirious, muttering the rhyme he knew so well:

"…weak of mind … traps the greedy … creeps and crawls …"

Mr Smith felt a fever clawing at his throat as the words marched through his head.

She wakes! The Sideways Lady comes for me.

PART II

London, today

6

The Clock Shop

There are parts of London visitors never see, and parts of London Londoners rarely see. Old streets. Forgotten streets.

Smith & Son was on one such street. A clockmaker, watchmaker, time fixer, or any variation thereof. The business had been there a great number of years, becoming a clock shop in the early twentieth century, when Thomas Smith converted part of his family home. A dark, narrow shop on a dark, narrow street and if you went to London hoping to have your timepiece fixed, the last place you'd go would be Smith & Son on Barricade Street. You'd simply never know it existed. Even so, it was not wholly unusual to see black-suited men strolling there to leave something for Mr Smith to fix.

These men would hand over their valuables and say something in the order of: 'It's for Her Majesty', or 'His Royal Highness', or 'The Right Honourable Whatisname.' Then, clasping a scrap of paper with a date intimating a week, sometimes two in advance, stroll back the way they'd come.

Mr Smith would place the broken clock or watch with other broken clocks and watches and, in time, fix it. He'd been in the trade for many years and loved everything about it. The solitude, the clocks ticking, his curious shop, and, up narrow steps, his tiny two-bedroom home. Mr Smith wasn't just Mr Smith, the clock man. He was Charlie Smith, son of Charles Thomas Smith. Jodie's father, grandad to Tess and Teddy.

Outside, a sunny day grew warmer. Inside, Mr Smith ate an apple and while he ate, marvelled at dust particles trapped in beams of filtered sunlight. A swirling, endless dust dance mesmerising him, making him feel comfortable, as though nothing from the outside world could disturb the peace he'd acquired.

The door of the shop opened, and the bell sang its happy jingle. Hesitant at first, Tess paused in the doorway. Every time she visited, she felt the little shop's magic, fearful one day the magic would dissolve, but that hadn't happened yet. She grinned at Grandad's familiar hunched figure.

He rose stiffly, his face matching his granddaughter's.

"At last. You're late!"

Mr Smith always accused Tess of being late. She never was and laughed. Tess felt safe with Grandad and dearly loved. She knew from the strength of his embrace. The bell jingled again, and they both turned to see the little boy standing there. He hesitated too, but it was nothing to do with magic. In silence, he surveyed the dingy space.

Mr Smith untangled himself from Tess. "Hello, Teddy. How lovely to see you."

Teddy didn't move.

"Is your mum there?"

"She couldn't park. She just dropped us and left," Tess said.

It was a familiar routine for Tess. Every holiday, since she was very young, she spent time in the clock shop. She was fifteen now and loved it more than ever. This was the first time with Teddy, and she was bitterly disappointed. From his sullen expression and persistent whining during the car journey, so was he.

"Well, come in, come in." Grandad flapped a hand.

He looked awkward, and Tess understood his turmoil. He'd always expressed astonishment at her continued enthusiasm for spending time in the shop, and the last time they'd spoken had voiced his fears about looking after Teddy, too. 'It's no place for a ten-year-old boy.' For one week, it was the only option.

"It's only a week. Nice for your mum to get a break." Grandad's smile faded.

Teddy had the decency to blush, but it went undetected in the gloom.

With a light touch on his shoulder, Grandad guided Teddy in. "By the end of the week, you'll know the name of every component of a watch." As soon as the words were out of his mouth, Mr Smith winced. "But if that's a bit boring, you can go through all my old comics and my special box of war medals."

"Were you in World War One?" Teddy gasped. He'd been learning about the Great War at school and from the way he eyed him up, it was obvious Teddy thought Grandad was old enough to have fought in it.

"He's not that old," snapped Tess.

The old man chuckled. "They're your great-grandad's medals and I'll show you later if you like."

Ecstatic, Teddy hopped up and down. Despite the melancholy of the shop, his blue eyes glinted. For someone who enjoyed collecting things, often without purpose, a war medal was a prized possession

"Okay, that's settled. Tess, why don't you take Teddy upstairs and show him where you're sleeping, then perhaps make some lunch?"

Lunch didn't bother Tess. She wanted to immerse herself in the shop, as she always did. Listening to ticking clocks. Watching Grandad work with the loupe attached to his head making his eye bulge.

"Come on, Teddy," Tess grumbled, climbing the narrow creaking stairs. She hated Mum for making Teddy come, hated Teddy for not putting up more of a fight, and hated herself for being unkind.

Sister and brother surveyed the small, yellow bedroom.

Tess claimed the bed that wasn't plagued by jutting springs and flopped down on it. The little bed by the window had always been hers. Familiar blue sheets bobbled with age. "You can sleep there," she pointed.

"This bed's lumpy and the sheets are funny," Teddy whined.

"Did you bring your sleeping bag like I told you to?"

Teddy scowled in reply. Muttering, Tess grabbed his holdall and rummaged through the contents. She found three well-worn cuddly toys, various gadgets, Spiderman pyjamas, and a multitude of socks. In a corner of the holdall, Tess found a screwed-up pair of pants. She wrinkled her nose. "Teddy! You've packed twelve pairs of socks and one pair of pants. Gross."

Teddy's scowl deepened, his bottom lip drooping in a pout.

"Come on. You hungry?"

"Can I have chips?"

Tess swallowed a sigh and led Teddy through to the little kitchen. She was used to its size and the lack of gleaming appliances, but this time she saw it through his eyes. Much like the rest of the house, the room was faded and old-fashioned with an added air of despondency. A sticky film wrapped itself around door handles and plastered cupboard doors. Years-old grime. Ingrained. Part of the fixtures and fittings. Cups and plates sparkled clean, but all were chipped. Scuffed paintwork, the window frame peeling with age. Tess hoped Teddy wouldn't look up and see the network of cobwebs making the ceiling light appear fluffy.

The shoebox freezer was devoid of chips, so Tess made Teddy a cheese sandwich. A poor substitute, resulting in more whining. As a result, the bread suffered.

"There's no garden," Teddy complained, gazing out the window.

"It is a garden, Teddy. Just without grass."

"I'm bored."

"Sometimes you have to make an effort *not* to be bored."

"I wish I could have gone with Mum."

Tess clattered the butter knife into the sink and stood beside Teddy. He was tall for his age and bony. All knees and elbows. She nudged him. "It's normal for people to go on honeymoon without their kids. It's only a week."

"Do you like Ivor?" Teddy turned to Tess, blue eyes misty with tears.

Tess thought of Ivor and his pale, puffy face. She wasn't sure if she liked him. Always busy doing things without ever achieving much. She grinned at Teddy and kept her feelings to herself.

"He's okay. He's not Dad, but he's okay."

"I wished we could have gone to Denmark to visit Dad."

"Yeah, well …" Tess dropped her arm, blew hot breath onto the window, and drew a sad face on the steamed-up glass. "It's cold in Denmark."

"Dad probably doesn't love us much anymore, anyway."

Tess stared at Teddy. With his blond hair and blue eyes, he looked like Dad, but Teddy had no memory of him living at home. Dad had left a year or so after the accident, when Teddy was two and Tess was seven. To Teddy, Dad was a stranger, but so much more to Tess. She saw eyes glinting behind round glasses, the shadow of whiskers, the prickly feel when she kissed his cheek. She remembered silly jokes and laughter, the terrible silences, and tears too. Despite being young, it came as no surprise when Dad left, anger and guilt a malignant tumour devouring them all. Without Dad, progress was made. Life resumed.

Grandad helped Tess understand the difficulties within her parents' marriage, much like he taught the complexities of a working timepiece. In the quiet of his little shop, she flourished. Healing inside, even if scars remained, blemishing her flesh.

"I think Dad loves us so much it's easier for him to just stay away." Tess drew a heart, then went back to the bread and cheese. "Tell you what, we'll go together if you like. When you're a bit older."

"Really?"

Tess smiled, savouring the truce, hopeful the week may not be so bad after all.

Teddy went back to finger-drawing on the window while Tess sliced cheese. She heard the jingle of the shop bell downstairs and felt at home.

"Someone's there."

Tess peered over Teddy's shoulder. "Where?"

"I saw something. Over there. Someone walking about." Teddy pointed beyond the small, grey square of concrete below.

"Something or someone?" Tess frowned.

Teddy shrugged, eyes still searching for whatever it was he'd seen.

"Someone funny. She looked at me."

"She?"

Tess scanned outside. Only wasteland beyond the courtyard. Or the dump, as Mum referred to it. *The dump*. There was another name Tess couldn't remember. The dump was an odd area, nestled away in the middle of London, but not a car or house in sight. Somewhere bleak that always looked the same to Tess, a world outside of

31

normal time. A strange place she'd always chosen to ignore.

Tess heard an echo of Nan's words and repeated them to Teddy. "It's not safe out there. You mustn't step foot outside the gate."

Teddy pressed his nose against the glass, pointing again. "What's that? In the distance."

"An old, ruined building. Dangerous."

Tess went back to the sandwiches, satisfied she'd dealt with Teddy's curiosity, but she was wrong. If she could have seen inside his mind, she would have seen the flat landscape was the moon and he stood amid the grey. An intrepid astronaut. There was something else too, flushing him with warmth and intrigue. Treasure glinting from the ground. Enticing.

7

A Phoenix

The shop's atmosphere felt alive. Time marked by the clamour of clocks, history caught within dancing particles of dust and bowed shelves packed with antique timepieces and aged historical volumes.

Sighing, Tess snuggled deeper into the arms of her favourite squishy chair. Gripped in her hands, *The Horror of Victorian England* creaking with age, pages brittle beneath her fingertips. Tess relished the real-life horror of the Dickensian era.

"Is Teddy okay, do you think?" Grandad asked.

"I'll check on him soon."

Grandad creaked as he leaned back in his chair. "I rarely had to worry about you. You're comfortable here. Part of the furniture."

Content, Tess breathed in the familiar smell. Part of the furniture was exactly how she felt. She stretched. "Was I always like that?" *After the accident. When nothing made sense and pain was a constant companion.*

In the gloom, Tess saw the glint of intelligent eyes. Grandad had never been afraid to discuss that time with her, raking over gory details, explaining why she'd emerge stronger than her peers. A phoenix, he'd called her. She believed him and eventually felt the change within herself. With surprising maturity, Tess knew who she was on the inside. The noise of the outside world, a nuisance, exhausting at times, but without influence. Alone at night, she sometimes fancied the steady beating of her heart was the ticking of a clock. The notion filled her with certainty. One day, she'd be a horologist. Her destiny was in the poky little shop smelling of oil and dust and old books.

"Even as a baby, you were watchful, methodical, and rather fierce."

"You mean I never smiled much?" Tess sniggered. She knew she'd been a sullen child. Had seen plenty of photographic evidence over the years.

"I could make you laugh."

"Dad, too."

Tess nestled deeper and returned to the yellowing pages of her book. She flicked over a page. An image drew her attention; a derelict building standing against a grey backdrop. Something about it stirred her inside. "*Thorncross Asylum*," she whispered, reading beneath the old photo. Peering closer, she saw the building wasn't derelict but partially destroyed by fire. A tingle ran along her spine.

"Grandad, what was the name of the old building way out in the middle of the dump?"

"Goodness me. Let me think. Thornfield?"

"Thorncross."

"That's the one."

Tess lowered her eyes again. Horrified. The opposite page contained information about the asylum, including the year it burned down and the estimated loss of life. She gulped and turned the page. More pictures. The asylum caught in bright flames licking a sombre sky, the smoking remains, and a full-size picture of a doughy-looking woman with small, piercing eyes. *The Matron.*

She lifted the book closer, peering into cold eyes. A stern, heavyset figure, the Matron had sloping shoulders, dangling hands, and fat fingers. A chain looped around her expansive waist, and keys rested against her hip. Tess imagined thick fingers working the keys, locking out light and hope. An object resembling a truncheon hung against the Matron's other hip. *A cudgel for controlling inmates.* Around her neck, hung a cross. A prickle of unease in Tess morphed into the certainty that this woman was no Christian.

Tess closed her book, went to the picture window, and gazed out at the narrow street. If she squinted, she could be in Dickensian London. The cobbles. The smog of a warm day quietly simmering. She often wondered if she was born in the wrong era, but Victorian London was brutal. The poverty and workhouses. The Matron. Tess pictured the woman wielding her cudgel and shivered.

"How's school?"

"Fine." Tess pictured Rav and grinned at her reflection. He'd fallen into step beside her on the last day of school and asked if she had plans for the holiday. She thought he might be leading up to ask if she wanted to meet, but the appearance of her best friend Amelia distracted her, and when she looked around for Rav, he'd gone.

"Any boys on the horizon?"

"Grandad!"

"I'll need to vet them first."

Tess sniggered, hiding her blush.

"And Mum?"

"Happy, of course."

"Good. She deserves to be happy."

Tess muttered a reply and tensed. She closed her eyes, focusing on the reassuring sound of ticking, perfectly timed with her beating heart. The solitude of the shop and easy companionship of her accepting Grandad were fuel for Tess's soul. Few understood, Mum included.

"I suppose I should check on Teddy."

"You know, when you first fell in love with the shop, your nan was still alive, and it was much less dreary."

"It isn't dreary!" Tess shrugged. Draped in gloom, the shop *was* dreary. And mysterious.

The old man reclined, creaking in his Edwardian chair, the seat covered in green velvet worn yellow in patches. He rubbed sandpaper hands together. "You used to love the Magic Drawer. Perhaps Teddy will too."

"Fine. I'll drag him down here and he can spoil my day." Tess stomped past Grandad, the harsh sandpaper sound jarring.

"He's probably afraid of losing his mum."

Tess faltered, one foot on the bottom step.

"Just a thought," Grandad mumbled.

Tess chewed her lip, feeling an unwelcome surge of turmoil at his words. Grandad was right, of course. The boyfriend was now stepdad, and the first thing he'd done was whisk Mum away. She'd chosen Ivor over Teddy.

"Yeah, well, I lost her years ago." Tess clumped up the stairs, irritation sparking.

"I think she probably feels the same, Tess."

Tess felt a jolt and a surge of remorse. The wise old man was right. She'd made no secret of the fact she'd prefer to live with her father in Denmark. Was the tension between herself and Mum all her fault? Should she be trying harder to conform, become the daughter Mum wanted her to be, instead of rousing displeasure by wearing 'ugly' boots and having 'straggly' hair? She took a breath. Perhaps she could begin by trying to be a better older sister.

Upstairs, bathed in a happy beam of sunlight, Teddy lay on his tummy on the front room floor.

"What you doing?"

Teddy scrambled to his knees. "Grandad said I could! I'm looking at his medals."

Tess knelt on the floor, the threadbare carpet rough against uncovered legs. She wriggled onto her bottom. Teddy copied.

"Show me."

Teddy handed Tess a silver star-shaped medal that felt solid and heavy.

"Very cool."

"There's more." Teddy scooped them up, metal clanking. His eyes gleamed.

"Why don't we ask Grandad about them later? He'd love to tell you."

"You really love Grandad a lot, don't you?"

"Of course. He's Grandad!"

"But you prefer it here."

Teddy coaxed the medals into lines, fingertips gliding across the patterned surfaces. Tess watched him, but he kept his eyes downcast. What was she supposed to say? She *did* prefer the poky little shop and Grandad's dim flat to being home with Ivor, Mum's nagging, and an annoying younger brother.

She stretched out her legs and looked around the tired little room. Grandad was right. Nan made the place brighter. Colours faded after she died, and age now clung to the fabrics and walls, but Tess loved it even more. This was the place where she could be herself and despite all the clocks and watches scattered everywhere, time never mattered.

"I do prefer it here. I want to fix clocks one day. At home, I have to tidy my room and go to bed on time. Come on, leave the medals. You'll be amazed at the treasures hidden in the shop." Tess walked away, not wanting to force Teddy to follow and trying hard to care.

Back downstairs, she picked up her book, flicking to a chapter on *Macabre Practices and Beliefs*. Minutes passed, then Tess heard Teddy's footfall on the stairs. She looked up, waiting for him to appear, but he stayed hidden within the narrow staircase's gloom.

Tess cleared her throat. "Grandad. Did you know when a child died in the Victorian era, the family would pay a photographer to take pictures?"

One eye huge behind his loupe—a circle of magnified glass attached to a metal frame and secured with a fabric strap around his head—Grandad peered at Tess and linked graceful fingers across his tummy. "Tell me more."

Tess raised her voice. "It gets worse. For instance, if I died, Teddy would have to have his photo taken with me. The photographer would probably make him put his arm around my cold, dead shoulders. Can you imagine?" Tess affected a horrified shiver.

Teddy popped out from the shadows. "Is that really true?"

"Yep. There are pictures. Come and look."

Teddy weaved between the obstacles in the crowded shop and perched on the arm of Tess's chair. He reached out and touched the glowing white faces and blank, staring eyes of the dead. "Are they really, really dead? Dead-dead?"

"Yep. Dead-dead!"

Grandad chuckled. "Horrible."

"Your eye looks funny." Teddy marvelled at the spectral eye.

"Come and try it."

Teddy weaved to the worktable and allowed Grandad to fix the loupe in place and tighten the strap. Teddy turned to Tess, a wide smile stretching his face. "I'm watching you," he chirped.

Tess poked her tongue out.

Grandad held up a small mirror so Teddy could see his huge, blue eye. He giggled. "Like a monster's eye!"

"Now then, I need help to make ready a *very* important clock. Might you be able to assist, Teddy? Her Royal Highness will be grateful."

Teddy quivered in his seat, eyes growing wide. "The Queen?"

"Not quite, but a princess. Tess, if you could produce the Magic Drawer."

Tess stroked the green inlay of the monstrous walnut desk, tracing aged scars with her fingers. "The Magic Drawer contains all the missing parts of every watch and clock ever made," she said.

Two pairs of blue eyes sparkled in her direction. Secrets were being shared.

Tess jiggled the discreet drawer and with a judder and sigh, the desk released its treasure. She carried it over and placed it down on the workstation. "The Magic Drawer."

The drawer was a jumble. Full of screws, dials, springs, nuts, washers, and hands, in varying sizes, some encrusted with jewels. Teddy smiled. A wide, crooked smile.

Grandad scratched his whiskery chin. "I've managed to fix the princess's grandfather clock, but it won't do at all if it breaks before she receives it, so I require a rubber band."

"Rubber band?" Covering his mouth, Teddy giggled.

Face solemn, Grandad held out three silver tubes. "These are the pendulums, but they're delicate. A band will secure them, don't you think?"

Teddy studied the drawer's contents, then grappled among the treasures. "Found one!"

"A red one too. I think the princess will be more than happy with the choice of colour. And now you know the secrets of the Magic Drawer, you must feel free to explore its contents whenever you choose." Grandad peered at Teddy from beneath unruly eyebrows, then winked. The little boy winked back, his face lighting in the glow from the Magic Drawer. Or perhaps beneath Grandad's loving gaze.

Time didn't travel too quickly in the old clock shop, but the week disappeared behind them. Maybe it didn't disappear entirely, but went out to the side, where it lingered full of combined energy. Like the crackle of electricity. A tingling, constant sense of anticipation.

8

The Sideways Lady

Inside the old clock shop, nothing changed. Teddy grew accustomed to the gloom and quiet and played without complaint. He climbed behind furniture, reached under beds, found prizes in the dark. Broken parts of forgotten clocks. Dust-coated treasures.

Without giving it much thought, one day, he said, "I saw that funny lady again."

Tess looked up from her book.

Grandad's eyebrows knitted together in a frown. Working fingers stiffened. "What funny lady?"

Teddy darted a nervous look at Tess. "She looks like those pictures, and she's got lots of clothes on. Like cloaks."

"What pictures?"

"The dead people."

Tess gulped. She snapped her book shut and heard its spine creak. Across the shop came the sound of a low moan. She jumped up. "Grandad?"

"Did you know about this?" he croaked.

"Teddy saw something over the dump the first day we were here."

Tess dragged a stool across the room and sat down. Grandad shook, his face a mask of fear. *It's nothing,* Tess told herself, but could see it was something. When Grandad spoke, everything changed.

"I must tell you something and need you to concentrate because it sounds like made up stuff. Fantasy."

Grandad gazed ahead, vacantly. Instinctively, Tess reached out for Teddy, but her fingers fluttered too far from his.

"There's a place called Sideways. It's always been there. You call it the dump, but it's much more than that." Grandad shuddered to a stop and ran a big hand across a thinning scalp. Tufts of grey hair stood on end, lending him the look of a madman.

A memory formed. Tess stood at the back gate, gazing Sideways. Afraid, she squirmed, revolted by the smell, but Nan clutched her hand until it hurt. Tess tugged free. Nan locked the gate, the back door, too, keeping Sideways and its stink away.

"Nan told me about Sideways a long time ago. She said I should never go beyond the gate, but I never wanted to." Tess wrinkled her nose.

"What's out there?" asked Teddy.

Agitated now, Grandad leaned forward and held Teddy's gaze. "It's what I'm trying to tell you. Sideways is bad. It takes your soul." Tired and frail, he slumped in his chair, a changed man from moments before. He glanced at Tess. "All these years without worry. You've never wanted to do anything more than stay here in this shop, but Teddy wants to explore. Am I right, Teddy?"

Teddy nodded, feeling like he'd done something wrong. He couldn't stop his mouth from tilting downward.

"Promise me you won't go out of the gate."

Teddy nodded.

"I'm not angry with you. Just scared."

Every clock in the little shop clamoured to be heard. Tess felt a chill coiling around her spine. "You're frightening Teddy," she muttered.

The old man stared at her with a haunted expression and deep lines she'd never noticed before. But his blue eyes were bright and clear as ever. "He should be frightened, Tess, because if he's seen her ..."

"Who?"

A second passed. Maybe two. A clock tick.

"The Sideways Lady."

"Who's that?"

Teddy's eyes grew wide. He looked pale and afraid. Tess stood, but Grandad was reciting a poem, mesmerising Teddy. Even the ticking hushed. The words sounded unnatural. A chilled warning. *The Sideways Lady comes for me.*

"Come on, Ted." Making a feeble attempt at laughter, Tess tugged at her brother's small hand. "He won't sleep tonight, Grandad!"

But no one was listening.

"Who is she, Grandad?" Teddy asked again.

"I don't know. Not exactly." Grandad closed his eyes and his mouth dropped open. Tess glimpsed the tarnished metal of sunken fillings as the seconds passed.

She reached to touch him. "Grandad?"

His eyes flew open. For a moment he looked stricken, then he fixed Teddy with a cold gaze.

Tick-tock.

The old man shuddered. "If you've seen her, it means she's seen you."

9

Oscillator

"**D**'you think Grandad's gone mad?" Teddy whispered into the dark.

"I don't know." Tess had never seen the old man so agitated and uneasy, and the rediscovered memory at the gate made her that way, too. She listened to her brother's breathing for a while. "Are you asleep?"

"No."

"You scared?"

"A bit."

Tess propped herself up. "Look, whatever happens, we're safe here, okay? Just don't go out there, Teddy."

For a while it was silent in the little yellow room. Tess closed her eyes, then she heard movement and Teddy spoke again.

"Tess?"

"Yes."

"Do you believe there's a Sideways Lady?"

Tess stared at the ceiling. At numerous cracks that looked like something had clawed through concrete and plaster. Peering through the dark, she turned to face her brother, making out the gleam of his eyes. "I don't know. Maybe. I won't let anything bad happen to you."

She thought of all Grandad had said and the way he said it. Tess had never once ventured beyond the back door, except for that one time with Nan, but she knew there was something out there. She'd seen it in Nan's eyes. That night, she saw it in Grandad's eyes too.

"Tess?"

"Yes."

"Can I get into bed with you?"

Tess sighed, not relishing the thought. The bed was narrow, and Teddy would grow hot and sweaty.

"Please?"

"Okay."

Sometime after midnight, with a full bladder, Teddy's gangly arms and legs in every direction, and sleep determined to elude her, Tess gave up and climbed out of bed. She crept from her room, heading to the toilet in darkness. A shaft of light oozing from beneath the kitchen door reminded her of melted butter on burned toast. She ignored her desire to pee and opened the door. Fully dressed, Grandad slumped at the shabby table amid several bits of clock.

"That's a mess."

He gasped and Tess lay a reassuring hand on his arm.

Grandad arranged a mountain of treasure before him. "I think Teddy's rather struck by the contents of the Magic Drawer. I did say he was allowed to take as much as he could carry, so long as he puts it all back."

Tess dropped into a small wooden chair. "He's not too good at that part. Sorry for the mess."

"I'm glad he's found something he enjoys."

Tess watched expert fingers form another peak. Uneasy silence hovered. A bulb blinked.

"Are you okay, Grandad?"

"I feel old and tired. Tried calling your mum. I want her to come back early and take you home. It's not safe here."

"She's on a cruise. She can't come back even if she wanted to, and you mustn't worry her. Don't tell her any of this. She'll think you're mad."

"Do you think I'm mad?"

"I think you're bonkers. Always have."

The light blinked again, and Grandad slumped further, his face ashen. "We mustn't leave Teddy alone. He's young and impressionable, easily lured." The old man shuddered and jostled bits of clock, destroying the peaks.

"I'll watch him. Make sure he doesn't wander off alone."

"I remembered some more of the rhyme."

Tess felt trapped in the little kitchen with the blinking light, but Grandad was oblivious to her discomfort.

He made fists with his hands, turning his knuckles white. "*Entices the child ...*"

Tess was hot and thirsty. She stood up and reached for a glass. It was chipped on the rim, as most were. Ancient pipes clanked and groaned at the gush of cold water. Tess filled the glass and flopped back down. She took a gulp, enjoying the cold coating her tongue and throat.

"Where does she come from? The Sideways Lady. What is she?"

Grandad still toyed with the shimmering litter strewn across the table. He picked up a thin gilt strap and wiggled it back and forth. A small gold snake.

"Do you know the history of the burned building in the distance, Tess?"

"Thorncross Asylum."

"Of course. The old book."

Grandad put the gold strap down and nudged it, as though trying to make the snake come alive. "Nervous anxiety was considered a mental ailment, you know. And post-natal depression. Those poor women. Hundreds of them, tortured."

"By the Matron." Tess saw the woman's pallid face and rodent eyes. Saw the cudgel swinging at her hip.

"The Matron, yes—"

"That was over a century ago. *Are you saying the Sideways Lady's a ghost?*"

Tess didn't believe in ghosts. She wanted to laugh, to swipe the treasures from the table, but cold dread kept her silent and still. The bulb blinked.

Grandad shook his head. "Nan believed the souls of those women lingered after the fire, and the chaos spread and became Sideways. Somewhere that isn't forwards or backwards. Sounds silly, I know, but Sideways is a diversion, luring you from your true path. Once you go Sideways, it gets inside and changes who you are." Grandad's doleful laugh puckered his face with worry, ageing him.

"But what about *her*? The woman Teddy saw—"

"A manifestation of madness or evil, I don't know. Nan talked to friends. Tried to understand. She felt *responsible*, you know?" Grandad drew breath, lines on his flesh deepening. Or perhaps it was shadows caused by the flickering bulb distorting an old face, forming a grotesque mask.

"You need a new bulb," Tess croaked.

He sat motionless. The gold snake too. Tess picked at a fingernail.

"This entity slumbered for years, until one day, a Knocker-Upper woke it up. Sideways became its home." Grandad regarded Tess with haunted, hooded eyes.

Tess took another sip of water, feeling the cruel edge of the broken glass against her lip. She didn't know what to make of the story. Like a fairy tale. An original Brothers Grimm version. Sinister, with spilt blood and malevolent shadows.

"Knocker-Uppers. I saw a picture of one, a woman with a pea-shooter. They woke the workers. The poor who couldn't afford alarm clocks," Tess said.

"Pea-shooters or long sticks. An efficient way of rousing the masses. The Knocker-Upper was a little too good at her job."

Tess gripped the old man's hand. Such a big hand for someone so skilled with the tiniest of tools. She hoped to reassure him, ease his worry as he'd so often done for her, but his hand was motionless, cold. Or was it her own hand that was cold?

He glanced up, wise eyes misty with tears. "I'm sorry. I never liked to think about it. Even when Nan was alive, she knew never to broach the subject. It was easier to pretend Sideways didn't exist if I didn't think about it and, of course, I never believed it could hurt me or anyone I loved." His lips wobbled as he pulled a large handkerchief from his pocket and dabbed his eyes.

"Did you ever try selling the land, so it wasn't yours to worry about?"

Big shoulders sagged. "It's attached to the shop. If I sold the land, I'd have to sell the shop. A long time ago, I hired a lawyer to go through the paperwork, but it cost lots of money and told me what I already knew."

Tess wasn't sure what to say. It was too much to deal with and the hour was late. The clock on the wall told her it was past 2am. She was cold and still needed to pee.

"It's late, Grandad. Why don't you try to get some sleep?"

He smiled a ghost of a smile. "You are a wonderful granddaughter and will grow up to be a lovely young woman." His words carried sudden warmth.

Tess blushed.

"And despite what you think, and how sometimes she may not show it, your mum is proud of you."

"I know." Tess smiled. Deep down, she thought it was probably true. "Come on then. Bedtime."

Her fingers hovered over the light switch as Grandad climbed stiffly to his feet.

"Do you know what the most vital component of a clock is?" he asked.

Tess walked back to the table and scanned the clock parts. All familiar to her and all neatly labelled in an image inside her mind. With a smug grin, she plucked a tiny piece shaped like a tuning fork. "The oscillator. Without it, the clock can't work. And this is quartz crystal. For a quartz clock."

Grandad beamed. "I'm rather excited at the prospect you might be the first ever female horologist in the Smith family line."

Tess placed the oscillator back on the table and flicked off the light. The bulb fizzed with relief.

"Except my name's Marken."

"True."

"And the name over the shop is Smith and Son."

"Also, true."

The old man chuckled, and Tess felt a rush of affection. She hugged him.

"Go to sleep and try not to worry," she said.

He winked. "Yes, dear. Church tomorrow, so I shall see you both at midday."

Grandad pecked Tess's cheek and disappeared inside the darkness of his room, but not before a faint, musty odour escaped. She winced and wondered if it remained untouched, with lace doilies and perfume bottles gathering dust. She wondered if there might still be a book on the bedside table with Nan's watch resting on top. Tess touched her hand to the door and listened, but the room was silent. She imagined Grandad lying still, staring at the ceiling. She faltered. He was scared and a little lost, which made her a little less scared.

Tess crept to the bathroom. She wasn't afraid of the dark and fairy tales weren't real. At least, that's what she told herself. In the poky little room, she stared at her reflection, the only light coming from a streetlamp outside. In the mirror, her face had a ghostly tinge. Eyes appearing sunken and black. Dark shadows surrounded her. She gulped. *Nothing to be afraid of.*

Dashing back to bed, Tess imagined ghouls chasing her. Afraid, after all.

10

Into the Void

Tess woke the next morning stiff from the springs of Teddy's bed and feeling like she hadn't slept. She squinted across the room at her bed, expecting to see Teddy fast asleep, but the bed was empty. Groaning, Tess turned, but sleep faded with her dreams.

Finding it impossible to find comfort on the springs, she gave up trying and got out of bed. It was chilly and she hadn't brought her dressing gown. Tess quickly picked through her clothes and dressed. Sunday. Only three more days without Mum and new stepdad. Tess wondered if Mum would want to change their surname. Tess liked the one she had. It was unusual and gave her a connection to Dad.

Half-asleep and yawning, she stumbled into the kitchen, scooping up scattered clock pieces to store in the pouch of her jumper. She didn't trust Teddy to return them. She wondered how Grandad had slept. Whether or not the Sideways Lady was real, he believed in the story. Tess imagined him in church, praying for something ungodly. She gazed out of the window. Always so bleak. An unchanging canvas. Except something was out there. She saw a red and blue flash, pressed her nose to the glass, and blinked. The colour disappeared.

Sideways was awash with grey. Nothing more. The window steamed and her tummy rumbled. Tess turned her back, boiled the kettle for tea, and toasted bread, but jitters chilled her flesh. Unable to resist, she glanced outside at the empty terrain. Not a single bird swooped across the sky. Odd. Eerie.

Steam swirled around the kitchen and the kettle switched off. Tess made tea. She couldn't help herself and went back to the window. Greyer grey. Interminable, it seemed. Could the Sideways Lady really be out there? Watching. Waiting. *What had the rhyme said?* Enticing the child.

"You won't have Teddy," Tess mumbled.

The toast popped and made her jump, but something else had caught her attention. In the drab courtyard below, a glint of something shining, a trail disappearing beneath the gate. The glass steamed up again, and the trail disappeared. Tess blinked and wiped away condensation. *Only my imagination.* She sipped tea. Funny how she'd never once been tempted to open the gate and venture outside, even if there was a shining trail to follow. Maybe if she was younger …

Entices the child.

Tess put her mug down, her shaking hand slopping tea over the rim. Liquid pooled on the scuffed table. Despite terror sprouting inside, she resisted the urge to scream for Teddy. She took a breath and clutched a chair to steady herself.

"Teddy?" Silence.

Tess left the tea and unbuttered toast and went to the small front room. The sun shone through the window, dappling beams of light on the carpet. Grandad's box of medals was out again, but Teddy wasn't there. The bathroom door stood open. Teddy's red toothbrush sat in the sink.

Tess knocked on Grandad's door. More silence. "Grandad?" Nothing. She flung open the door and glanced inside, reluctant to intrude. The room was impeccable, ordered. Nan's presence lingered, even her smell. Tess inhaled before tugging the door closed.

"Please be downstairs. Please be downstairs," Tess chanted, hurtling down the narrow stairs, almost losing her footing.

The shop was dark and still. No sign of Teddy. Tess screamed his name, yanking open the door to the original kitchen—a narrow galley with a rusting sink. Empty. Teddy would never use the downstairs toilet. Too many spiders and a cracked toilet seat that pinched. Tess checked anyway. Empty.

She ran back upstairs, breathing ragged. Perhaps he went to church with Grandad, Tess thought, knowing he never would. She dashed inside their shared bedroom, hot tears running down her cheeks. Toys and gadgets littered the floor, and it was colder than it should be, like a presence was in the room with her. Something breathing cold air. Or someone. Tess's heart pounded, but she grew still. The faded pale yellow pattern on the wall now looked grey. *Had it always been so?* She gulped, dread spiralling inside. Closed her eyes. Listened. No sound, no movement, but a smell she recognised. Only slight, but unmistakable. *Teddy.*

Tess spun around. He was there somewhere. In some illogical way. Standing in front of her. Screaming for help. "I'll find you," she choked.

Tess sat on her bed, fighting socks that suddenly seemed too small. Her mind whirred with possibilities, but one thing was certain. She felt it with terrible clarity. Sideways was real, which meant *she* was real, too. Tess wiped a shaking hand across her face. *Why had no one warned them? What was she supposed to do?* Grandad was in church praying, but Tess knew prayers may not be enough.

Fearful, she whimpered, but there was no time to waste. She'd told Teddy she wouldn't let anything bad happen to him and had meant it. Now was the time to act, not wait, cowering for Grandad or the police. She tugged on her boots and marched downstairs. Teddy needed her, and she wasn't about to let him down.

Clocks clamoured at her approach, dust swirling in endless spirals, but Tess was oddly calm. Resolute. She pushed open the back door and stepped into the barren courtyard. The only colour came from an orange ball and green can, both speckled with dirt. There was a reason Nan didn't bother with pot plants or flowers in the gloomy space. She hadn't wanted to give Tess a reason to step outside the shop, but Teddy had been lured, regardless.

She opened the gate, but the Sideways stink made her hesitate. She'd wait for Grandad. He'd know what to do. Tess closed her eyes and for a moment was on the moon, adventure before her. She clung to the vision. Teddy's vision. How could she wait?

Tess took a breath, clenched her fists, and stepped into the void. One step, then another. Changing her life forever.

11

Drowning

Assaulted by smell. Disarmed, overwhelmed, Tess tucked her nose into her jumper and trudged on.

She'd smelled something similar once before. She was young, and Mum had left her with elderly neighbour, Mrs Ingram, for an hour. A lifetime to Tess. The old lady gave her milky tea and fruitcake. She'd been kind, indulged Tess with sweets, but in her little kitchen, Tess endured a terrible nightmare in the shape of a cauldron of putrid stew restlessly simmering on the stove. Tess felt the smell upon her flesh, tasted it on her tongue before Mrs Ingram called on her to stir the concoction. Lumps of meat bobbed around. Miniature monsters in a grey swamp. The image and the stink stayed with her for weeks.

Now it resurfaced, invading Tess's nostrils and eyes. She imagined being sucked into something. Kept looking back to reassure herself the gate was still there. She did her best to ignore the ominous feeling that the grey would swallow it up. Tess walked a while, then stopped to think. Someway distant was the old institution. She was certain Teddy wouldn't have gone that far. Perhaps he was back in the shop already, nestled in the squishy armchair. Looking through her book, staring at the white faces of dead children.

Tess looked around. The silence of Sideways engulfed her and a memory resurfaced. Standing at the gate with Nan clutching her hand. 'Sideways is forever,' she'd said.

The moaning of a teasing, sombre wind surrounded Tess. She called out for Teddy, but her voice skimmed into the distance, like a pebble dancing across water. She might as well be in the middle of the ocean.

She ploughed on, ignoring the eerie silence, listening to her own thoughts, remembering Teddy. The smell wasn't helping, nor the cold. She plunged her hands into the pouch of her jumper. Fingers caught pieces of watch and clock, giving Tess an idea. She gathered a handful and dropped them to the ground. A watch face. Small springs. An escape wheel. The quartz oscillator glinted at her from the flat, solid earth. A mountain of treasure neatly arranged. A beacon for them both. The way home.

Several more steps, another glittering peak. The gold watch strap, snakelike in the dirt. As the institution neared, Tess left another mound of treasure. It was all she had. She hoped it was good enough. Too afraid to look towards home, Tess closed her eyes and listened. Like a heavy blanket, the smell wrapped around her. She imagined an army regulation blanket. Thick wool. Scratchy. Mrs Ingram's son had one of those. The boy smiling from a photo frame. She never spoke about her son, but Barney, her half-blind dog, used the blanket for a bed.

Tess opened her eyes, wishing she hadn't thought about Mrs Ingram. It made her think of the meat stew, made her imagine she was a piece of meat bobbing up and down, waiting to be devoured.

From the ground, a teddy bear peered through its one eye. Glad for the distraction, Tess scooped him up. The bear was ancient, sparse fur stiff with grime. Though filthy, a red ribbon around its neck stood out against the bleak landscape. Tess sat the bear on the ground, pointing one of his arms towards the first mountain of clock parts.

"If you see Teddy, you can show him the way home."

Hunched in her big jumper, she walked away from the bear and his accusing stare. The institution now offered hope. Something flickered in its shadow. The dull glow of fire. Tess traipsed towards the flames and the ruined building grew monstrous in her sight. One side was missing, gaping open, most of the roof collapsed. Stone posts jutted skywards. A skeletal hand, or the cruel, rotting teeth of a giant. Empty windows watched her crunch over crumbling bones of the building.

Tess edged closer to the fire, its heat and friendly crackle leaving her cold. She stared through the flames at the pile of rags opposite. Rags with unblinking eyes. She gulped but stepped closer. This wasn't the Sideways Lady.

"Hello."

"So, you came. I'm Mary."

The flames carried the stranger's voice with a crackle and spit. Tess wondered if she was dreaming, but then another smell besieged her, a 'bag of rubbish left out in the sun' smell.

"I'm looking for my brother."

"Can't help you."

"He's hiding."

Tess spun around. Wearing a tattered dress stood a little girl with bare feet and white, straggly hair. She was thin and small, her pinched face drained of colour.

"I'm Alice. Are you his sister?"

"Have you seen him?"

"I did before, but don't know where he is now." Alice squatted by the fire.

"I need to find him." Tess tried to keep the urgency from her voice. The atmosphere around the fire was one of calm. She couldn't imagine Mary or Alice leaping to her aid.

"Problem is, if he got scared and closed his eyes like I did, he'll go back home. Somewhere he feels safe. How old was he?"

Was?

"Ten," Tess stuttered.

"He'll be scared then and hiding. Here, but not here."

Tess perched on a slab of concrete, her legs shaky beneath her. "What do you mean? Here, but not here?"

Silent and watchful, Mary gawped. Tess wondered how the old woman could appear so contemptuous without saying a word. She faced Alice instead. Small and scrawny, she reminded Tess of a baby bird. Easy to break.

"His body is here, but when you shut your eyes, the soul departs. He won't want to come back here, because of *her*." Alice shrugged, twisting the ruined skirt of her dress in anxious fists.

"But you've seen him. Can't you show me?"

Another shrug. "You've walked through it. It's impossible to find things. The grey swallows you up."

"Why didn't you bring him here?"

"Like I said. Things disappear."

The fire shot out a blue flame, an accusing finger that startled Tess. She must be dreaming. An old crone hiding in frowzy rags. The birdgirl. Even the fire had a strange quality, dancing its own dance.

The wind moaned, and goosebumps popped across Tess's flesh. No dream. The cold was real, and Teddy was out there somewhere. She stood and squinted, trying to make out Mary's features. "Who are you?"

Mary clambered to her feet and hobbled around the fire. She narrowed her eyes at Tess, peering with a hint of disdain. "Told yer. I'm Mary."

"Yes, but—"

"Who I am is neither 'ere nor there. Worry about 'er. Learn. She don't like my fire, same as you."

Tess realised the woman wasn't old. She was ancient. Like a tree. Opaque, aged eyes held wisdom, but something else. Cold. Brutal. Understanding. Equally unsettling were the scores of fleas that hopped about her person.

"I just want my brother back."

"It's a trifle more complicated than that, I'm afraid."

"Of course it is." Tess sighed, begrudging the old woman and her intense gaze.

"She's been Mistress of time for too long and you're the one."

The old crone made no sense. Baffled, Tess shook her head. "I don't know what you mean and in case you didn't know, I'm fifteen!"

"No matter. You're here. Sideways, but not *really* Sideways. Like me."

Tess had no doubt the woman was mad, and yet, those eyes, the palest blue, lingering on Tess as though she might impart some ancient wisdom.

"How can I be Sideways, but not Sideways?"

"You still got your colour."

Tess turned to the little birdgirl. She'd spoken in her grey voice, a small smile on colourless lips. The child seemed so young, helpless. Was she alone with just Mary for company? A terrible thought that twisted Tess's insides.

"I don't understand," Tess choked, but thinking perhaps she did.

Alice toyed with the strands of her white hair. "Sideways takes the colour from your soul. Makes it cold inside. Like your bones are made of ice, but I can see your colour."

Tess recalled Grandad saying the same thing about Sideways taking part of the soul away, but why was she different? She turned to Mary to ask, but the old woman smirked, all knowing, and spoke with her gruff voice and unwelcome stare.

"You're Tess, from your toes to your nose. Wilful and heedful. No doubting who you are. You've suffered alone and I imagine you don't care what others think."

Tess felt irritation rising, but she fought against it. Disgusting as Mary was, with her odious breath and creatures hurtling across swathes of stinking rags, she would help Tess find her brother. She *had* to help.

"Mum calls me wilful. Makes it sound like it's a bad thing."

Mary wobbled her head, and wispy hair lurched. "Might save your life. Sideways takes the essence of a soul easily and quickly. Folk are all jumbled up inside. Like too many ingredients in a cake. Too much of themselves they don't know, but you and me, we don't change for no one."

What about Teddy's soul? Tess was too afraid to ask. *She's mad. Bonkers. Or I am.*

Mary smirked again. She scooped up her rags and strolled back to her side of the fire, mumbling as she went. The fire crackled, sounding like laughter.

Tess tried processing the notion of Teddy's soul separate from his body. It seemed ridiculous, but she'd smelled him. "I think Teddy was back at Grandad's. I'm certain he was."

"Then you need to bring him back here and tell him he *must* get back to his body." Alice's pitiful smile was meant to encourage, but Tess felt a stab of agony. She gulped, unable to speak or think, and turned to leave.

Mary stabbed the fire with her stick. "If you go now, she'll be waiting on your path. She's lurking out there. I can smell 'er. Wait, and when it smells right, go, and find him."

"Teddy can't wait!"

"Then go now. But she'll snatch you up."

Tess whimpered. "What will she do with me?"

"Depends. Sometimes she likes to keep pets, other times not. She don't much like boys, though."

"Pets?" Tess felt a stab of adrenalin at the thought of being the Sideways Lady's pet.

Mary sniffed. "If she wants to keep you like she kept Alice, you stay alive. Such as it is. I 'ave a feeling she'd like to keep you."

Tess was drowning. Once, as a little girl, she'd been caught in a sea current. Only a matter of seconds, but with water surging, filling her mouth, blinding her, she thought she'd drown. She had that feeling now and pictured Dad's strong arms reaching down, plucking her from the waves. But this time, he couldn't save her.

Tess shrugged off the memory. "So 'ow will I know? I mean, how will I know, if it smells right?"

"How does it make you *feel*? The Sideways perfume?"

Tess thought of Mrs Ingram's meat stew and shuddered. "Repulsed."

Mary nodded her agreement. "Umble-cum-stumble, but we're a rare breed. Folks what get tricked into coming Sideways *see* things that lure 'em. They don't use their nose. Don't stop to use their 'ead either."

"Lucky us."

"She travels far, visits other places, but when she's close, the stink turns you inside out. Gets inside your mind, strips you bare. Mark my words, she's not far."

Tess inhaled. Carried towards her, a scent that made her feel afraid. Not Mrs Ingram's stew, but the Devil's.

"So, what do I do now?"

"You wait. Time don't work the same 'ere. No time has passed."

Tess looked back towards home. Undulating grey. No gate. Nothing. Then she glimpsed the bear's red ribbon and, beyond that, a tiny glint of silver. She scanned the wilderness until the gate shimmered into view, an obscure drawing pinned against a bleak canvas.

Alice tugged Tess's arm. "Come on. Let me show you inside the asylum. If Mary said you shouldn't go yet, listen to her."

Tess gaped at the institution. The black-and-white picture from her book had chilled her. *Would phantoms lurk within the ruined walls?* "Is it haunted?" she whispered.

"Come and see."

Tess followed the little birdgirl, choosing to take her chances with the ghosts within rather than with the creature lurking without. Perhaps Alice was a ghost, too. If not, how long had she been stuck Sideways? How many years?

The thought of Teddy being stuck chilled Tess's bones. Growing old, but not old. Every day. Forever.

12

Dust and Stone Skeletons

The mouth of the old asylum yawned wide. As Tess trod upon the crumbling steps leading inside, she had a sense of walking back through time.

The entry hall had once been an expansive space. Lofty ceiling, tiled floor, imposing windows. A first impression for visitors. A charred desk slumped drunk. Tess pictured nurses in crisp uniforms. White to match their smiles. She pictured the Matron. Cudgel in hand, cross at her neck.

"Do you know about this place?" Alice asked in her grey voice.

"I read about it. It was called Thorncross Asylum."

Voices carried, echoes replying in whispers.

Tess wiped sweating hands, trying to work saliva into her mouth as Alice climbed over rubble towards the remains of a sweeping staircase. Somewhere nearby, something fell, exploding to dust.

Tess paused, eyeing a teetering pillar. "Is it safe?"

"It's stood like this for over a century. Just follow me."

Over a century. Did that mean—?

"Alice, how long have you been here?"

"Mary says if I'd been living my life, I'd be long since dead. My children, too."

The wide space of the entry hall seemed to close upon Tess. She wanted to wake, consign Alice to her dreams, but the little girl stood before her, a white wisp. "I'm sorry."

"Don't be. This is all I know. Memories come and go, but mostly this is it. Me and Mary."

They stood at the foot of the broken-up staircase. Despite the ceiling and most of the roof being open to the elements, the air was still and stale. Oppressive. Tess had visited ruins before, derelict castles, crumbled down old buildings. All of them with sprouting weeds, families of birds, nature reclaiming stone. The asylum was devoid of life and yet a presence lingered and shadows stirred. Tess felt an ominous wave of unease. "Does she come back here?"

"No. She's afraid. This was her prison all those years before she got woked up."

Tess gazed about, picturing the fire as it roared through the building. Mighty flames burning. Claiming lives. Fearful, she shuddered.

As though she saw it too, Alice whispered. "Mary says, when the asylum burned, *she* was born out of the madness, but she couldn't wake up. Sideways was alive with her soul, but while she slept, there was hope. Trouble was, she wanted to wake up *bad*, and she waited a long time."

"Mary said I was the one. Do you know what she meant?"

"Mary talks in riddles sometimes, but maybe …" The little girl faltered, shrugging.

"Maybe, what?"

"Someone needs to trick *her*. Send her back to sleep, but Mary don't know how, nor do I."

Tess baulked, panic rising. "*I don't know.*"

"Not yet." Alice grinned and skipped away.

Tess had the sensation of drowning again, but she cast aside her dismay and followed the colourless wisp. For now. When the time was right, she'd find Teddy and go home.

Sections of the staircase and the right-side balustrade no longer existed. Tess had an uneasy feeling the entire structure could collapse, but Alice climbed with the confidence of a goat. At the top, on solid ground, Alice turned left, leading Tess into a vast room with many black metal beds. Most of them overturned or upended, the bedclothes long gone. Towards the end was a single bed covered in blankets. The portion of roof above the room was intact, offering little protection from the outside.

"This is where I sleep." Alice's announcement was matter-of-fact.

Tess swallowed her anguish and tried to think of something hopeful to say without success. The room was cold and colourless. As though defiant, the air about her stirred. Invisible fingers poked, tugging at her hair. Someone whispered in her ear.

"What the—?"

"The kids are playing with you."

Tess spun around, but the room was empty. "Ghosts," she breathed.

"They're company sometimes."

On skinny, dirt-stained legs, Alice marched from the room. Tess stared, speechless. If she wasn't dreaming, she must have gone mad. She took a deep breath and felt saner than she ever had in her life, reaching out, touching stark walls, feeling the children's presence through stone and brick. They were everywhere. Watching her. Hiding. Tess wasn't afraid of them, but of the world she was in. She didn't want to be there. Not one bit.

Poised in the doorway, Alice waited. "Are you coming?" she called.

They clambered over rubble to the rear of the institution. Tess saw there'd once been sweeping gardens, statues, perhaps a pond. She imagined flowers growing in abundance. What the fire hadn't destroyed, Sideways had swallowed. Fallen trees of dust and stone skeletons all that remained. Beyond the ghostly garden, the landscape was flat and ash grey. They might have been inside the earth, a vast hole that went on forever.

Tess closed her eyes and saw the vibrant golds and reds of autumn, Grandad's favourite time of year, bringing life to dreary London. Even when smog and rain obscured the view, there was life. Birds. Colour. Noise. There was a sun and moon, and though rarely glimpsed in the city, stars. Celestial bodies of light. Twinkling eyes. Something to wish upon. What Alice endured was unbearable and Tess shuddered as Sideways moaned. If she ever got home, she vowed never to take anything for granted again.

Alice said Sideways was alive with the soul of the Sideways Lady, but Tess thought the emptiness *was* her soul. Malignant, with a hungry mouth. After her accident, after Dad had gone, Tess lost herself. On the outside, she was Tess. Smiling. Living life. On the inside, she felt herself eroding. She stood upon the precipice of a bottomless well but clung on. Now she imagined Sideways was the well. Empty and forever.

Tess reached out, hoping to feel something against her flesh. A sign of life. A change in the air. Alice copied the gesture. Her hand was small and pale. Faded, as though partially rubbed out. *Was she disappearing?* Tess scrambled to her feet and walked away, but Alice followed. They backtracked past the children's ward, along a narrow artery, splodges of mould staining the walls. They came upon a small room with filing cabinets burned to fragments of vicious metal. Disfigured remains of an immense desk lay dead on the ground, limbs askew.

A nightmare animal. Burned. Twisted. A pair of crooked reading glasses sat among the ruin, as if the crouching monster watched, a strip of charred cloth all that remained of a curtain hanging at an unbroken window.

"I don't like this room," Alice's nervous eyes flickered.

Tess felt it, too. An uneasy energy filling the space. She expected to see someone standing in the dark corner. Mad, unblinking eyes watching her, but the corners were empty. They looked out of the window, their bodies touching.

Tess scanned the void. "Can you see anything?"

Like shining silver thread, a tear glistened against Alice's pale cheek. "If I try really hard, I can see home and Mama waiting for me. If I close my eyes, she's waving and smiling. It's not real, of course, just my imagination, but it makes me happy."

"Can you see her now?" Tess whispered.

"No need to try today. You're here."

Alice wiped her tears and leaned against Tess with a sigh, but Tess felt anguished at her touch. Alice was a burden she couldn't cope with. She wanted Teddy back and needed Mum to be more than a figment of her imagination.

"I hope you find your brother, Tess."

Tess flinched, guilt and sorrow converging. She draped her arm across Alice's shoulders and the small frame snuggled closer.

"Is it true what Mary said before? That you don't listen to others, or do what others do?"

"I guess I just never bothered about fitting in." Tess knew that wasn't strictly true. She'd never known how to fit in. "I think being different means it's easier to get to know who you are on the inside." *Or was it the other way around? Did knowing who you were make you different?*

Tess endured therapy sessions to understand what made her tick, but ultimately, all the talking and reassurance did no good. She was cursed, or blessed, with having to fight, so rolled up her sleeves and got on with it.

"The problem is people have too much to say. It's easier to ignore them all." Tess laughed, feeling a wave of shame. She ignored Mum, too. Would things be any different if she were home now?

Alice waited for more. Held her breath. The voice of another would revitalise, or at least distract.

Tess sighed. "The world you knew has gone, and I doubt you'd recognise it. So much has changed for the better. Mostly. But it can be so tiring—"

"What's your job?"

"No work—kids don't have to work now—but it's a different kind of tired. Exhausting. Always trying to be the same as everyone else. Pretending you're not different when inside, everything feels completely upside down."

"Oh."

"I stopped trying in the end. Did my own thing." Tess knew she was unusual for enjoying time spent in a dusty old shop learning about clocks.

"Mary *was* right."

A howling wind churned the grey landscape, reminding Tess of the meat stew. *We're pieces of meat waiting to be eaten.* "Let's get out of here."

Together, they climbed down the staircase. At the bottom, Tess hesitated. The door stood open, but Sideways felt dangerous. Alive with *her* stink. Tess slumped on a crumbling step.

Nervously, Alice clutched at the material of her thin dress. "Did I say something wrong?"

"No! No, Alice. You didn't say anything. I'm sorry." How could Tess explain how she felt? No doubt trivial given their predicament, and yet in the bleakness of her surroundings and perhaps for the first time, Tess felt glad she'd endured the worst of times. All those dark days that had stretched into weeks and months. Staring inside herself, empty and afraid, every moment now perfectly fused together. She had survived. No. It was more than survival. She'd been reborn, and Mary was right. She didn't listen to the noise around her. All that did was chip away the foundations of who she was.

"The hardest thing is convincing people you're happy." Tess thought of her mother again, who was certain her only child couldn't possibly be happy spending so much time with a dusty old man in a dusty old shop.

Alice shuffled in the broken floor debris and bent to pick up a piece of rock. She turned it over and over in her fingers. Tess watched dust fall. A light sprinkling of ash. *Or bone.* Alice clambered across a section of wall and worked the stone against a sharp edge. She kept her eyes lowered as she whittled.

"I wanted to be better than everyone else. I thought I *deserved* to have a better life."

"There's nothing wrong with wanting things, Alice."

Haunted eyes lifted and stared. "I know, but you mustn't forget who you are, and that's what happened to me."

Tess felt the scar that clawed at her neck and knew she could never forget who she was. The scar was on the inside, too. *I'm the same through and through.*

Alice blew on her stone and inspected it. "Mary said Sideways lures people, preys on weakness. She said it should be called Blindways because you may as well be blind. That was me. Too ready to believe in something that wasn't real."

Another gust of wind rattled the asylum, and the huge front door creaked. Dust and dirt lifted, spiralling with the smell.

"What's she like, Alice? The Sideways Lady?"

Alice stopped whittling; the stone clutched in rigid fingers. All was silent. When she looked at Tess, her wide eyes were full of horror. "Getting lost Sideways is like being half-asleep, but there was always a glimmer of hope. There isn't any with her. She takes everything you are. She's what you fear and what you hate, and it's forever."

Tess's heart hammered in her chest. "I don't know what Mary thinks I can do."

"Mary thinks Sideways is your destiny, but if something's your destiny, it's not Sideways, so I don't understand."

Tess didn't understand either. She ached for Alice, but this wasn't her fight or her destiny. She squirmed inside, longing to be free from this child's gaze, her fragility.

Alice spoke as if she could read Tess's mind. "Don't feel too bad for me. I have Mary. I don't know what I would do without her, despite her smell."

Tess laughed. It seemed the right thing to do. "It's pretty bad!"

Alice placed her whittled stone on a natural shelf in the wall. Tess noticed the stone had taken on the shape of a head and body. Then she saw the other stones neatly lined up. Hundreds of them. A stone family. Tess turned away, swiping at tears before Alice could see.

Alice picked her way across the rubble of the entrance hall and beckoned Tess. "Something else to see. You can hold my hand if you want."

They stared down a narrow flight of stairs. An imposing metal door stood at the bottom, partially hidden in shadow. Blackened and buckled, but rigid against the crumbling doorframe. Their footsteps echoed as they crept down. Alice slithered through the gap and Tess followed, instantly feeling a cold draught sweep towards her. Gulping, she faltered.

"It's where they kept the really mad people," Alice whispered.

They edged along the gloomy corridor, passing many doors on either side. Metal doors with dark slits. Alice nudged one door open, and Tess went inside the cell. It was claustrophobic, the metal frame of a small bed jammed between two walls. If the women were unstable before, confined here for any length of time must have let demons in. A smell lingered. Filth. Rot. Blood. Tess's stomach lurched. One barred window, the size of a letterbox, would have given a torturous glimpse of sky, when once there'd been sky. Madness hadn't been driven out, but encouraged in. Women with post-natal depression had endured torture within these walls. *What was the term she'd read in her book? Morbid melancholy.* Unavoidable and terrifying, the metal rings fixed into stone, cruel manacles dangling.

Tess traced her fingertips over crude scratches on barren walls. "Those poor women."

"I hear them sometimes."

"Can we leave?" Tess couldn't bear the confined cell a second longer. She felt a presence, heard whispered screams, and anguished pleas. The women were long-since dead, but tortured souls remained alive. In purgatory.

Along the corridor, Tess paused, peering through a darkened slit of a closed door. She inhaled the muffled silence of the cell's despair. There was a lock, but no key and no handle. Tess lay her palm against the frigid metal. "After the fire, did anyone collect their bodies?"

"Nobody cared enough, so Mary said."

In silence, Tess and Alice left the institution. Tess looked back, glad to be free but affected by what she'd seen and felt. This wasn't just about Teddy and Alice. She glanced at the unbroken window, at the fabric hanging dolefully. She thought of the hard-faced Matron and knew the room had been her office. *And where the Sideways Lady dwelt, hidden in shadow.*

"I saw a photo of this place and there was something about it. Hard to explain, but I felt uneasy looking at it. I imagined evil spirits lurked inside—"

"Mostly just sad."

"Except for *her,*" Tess muttered.

Alice trembled and crumpled upon the top step, hiding her face. Tess sat beside her, noticing the little girl's bony knees scuffed and dark with dirt. She draped an arm around Alice's thin shoulders and was reminded of Teddy. He was skinny too. Tess's eyes filled with tears, but she wasn't sure whether it was the thought of her brother or Alice's plight. Weakness consumed her, like swimming through a dark, terrible sea.

For a moment, all was silent. Not even the wind howled. Then Alice spoke. "It took three peas to wake her."

"What?"

"The Sideways Lady. I knew something wanted waking up, but it took me three peas."

"You're the Knocker-Upper?" Tess was breathless.

"My Nan was one, and I used to go with her. In the end, she got gout, and I took over. Youngest Knocker-Upper in London, and the best. Until I waked *her* up."

"Why did you do it?" Tess stammered, ashamed. "I don't mean …"

"From the moment I took Nan's pea-shooter, it was going to be me. Besides, you can't imagine how it felt. In that moment I forgot everything I loved. A feeling swept me up and gave me hope. I imagined flying. Free from the dirt and fleas."

"Alice—" Tess took a breath, but she had no words.

Alice turned to Tess, the grey pools of her eyes beseeching. "I'm not a ghost, you know." She touched her chest and stilled for a moment, listening, gazing into emptiness. "I don't know what that makes me, though. I just wished it wasn't endless. Wish I knew that time was passing, and it would all stop one day."

"It will," Tess mumbled, feeling like the world's biggest fraud.

Even worse was knowing she planned to leave Sideways with no idea how'd she ever help Alice. Before the thought took hold and made her feel too much, the grey shifted around them. It stank less. Didn't feel so oppressive.

Tess hadn't realised, but the air had been thin. She filled her lungs and stood. "She's gone. Time to get Teddy back."

13

Goblins and Gallantry

Stranded in hellish limbo, or at the edge of a nightmare, then falling into its depths. That was Sideways. *Snatched breath. Bewildered mind. Weak body.* Had she been alone, Tess might have believed in the nightmare. Perhaps convinced herself she'd wake up and be free from its clutches. But she wasn't alone. The slight figure of the girl strode alongside. Trapping Tess. Torturing with her smile.

"You didn't have to come, Alice." Tess felt a rush of guilt. Alice had nothing better to do. "I mean, I'm glad you did."

Alice was unaware she was an unwelcome companion. "It's probably a good idea for me to come. Just to the start of your trail. It's easy to get lost here."

Tess didn't doubt, but wasn't she supposed to be different? *Hadn't Mary told her she was Sideways, but not Sideways?* Besides, Tess could already see the teddy bear's red ribbon standing out against stark grey. She glanced at Alice. A small, lost urchin. Bare feet, old-fashioned dress not much more than a rag.

"Aren't you worried *you* might get lost?"

Alice shook her head. "This part of Sideways is mine."

The idea horrified Tess. Was a part of Sideways designated for her, too? She tried shrugging off the implication, to have a normal conversation, but normal wasn't happening anymore.

"If this part of Sideways is yours, how did Teddy get here? And me?"

Alice looked thoughtful. "We had the same starting point, maybe? Mary would say, right place, right time."

"Right place, right time. Right." Tess drew breath. Normal was nowhere in sight. "So, where does the Sideways Lady disappear to, then? How big is Sideways?"

"Sideways is forever." Alice gazed up to where sky should be.

Tess stopped to look at the bleak, birdless space. An upside-down heaven where monsters might dwell.

"It's nothing and everything. Bigger than the world, Mary says, but the world will end one day. Sideways won't though. It will always be here."

The simplicity of Alice's words blew an icy draught through the middle of Tess. She grew scared. Not just for Teddy and herself, but for everyone. The whole of London and beyond. She picked up the pace, concentrating on her feet, reminding herself it wasn't her fight. Only Teddy was her responsibility.

They marched on, Tess's boots crunching over brittle ground. She noticed Alice staring. "You like my boots?"

Alice smiled. "I do."

It's not my fight. Oh, God. Don't let it be my fight. "Don't you have any shoes, Alice?"

"My shoes were old and broke apart. Mary says the soles of my feet have more wear than a tittle-tattler's tongue!"

Indifferent, Alice shrugged, but Tess had a lump in her throat, impossible to swallow. It was agony to dwell on Alice's hard-wearing feet. "Mum hates my boots. She thinks they're ugly." Tess couldn't suppress the scowl as an image of her mother's disapproving face hovered before her eyes. The clock inside her chest skipped. At least she had a mum.

"I don't really miss Mama anymore. It was so long ago, and my memories are broken up. Sometimes, it's hard to piece them all together."

"I'm sorry, Alice."

"Don't be. It's a good thing. Means it's easier to pretend this is all normal."

Not my fight. "Did you know Mary before?"

"Sort of. Everyone knew *of* Mary. She used to tell people about Sideways, but most people thought she was mad. Suppose she is a bit, and she definitely smells, but you get used to that."

"Smelly Mary," Tess mumbled, making Alice laugh. A strange sound in the unchanging, barren world draped around them.

Tess glanced at Alice and wished she hadn't. She was smaller than Teddy. More vulnerable. Ghostlike. Tess stumbled to a halt, willing herself to wake up, but cold fingers brushed her own. She sank to her haunches, gripping Alice's wasted arms.

"I wish there was something I could do. *Anything.*"

The little girl's smile tore at Tess's heart. "A cuddle would be nice,"

Tess held back a sob and wrapped her arms around Alice, wanting to transfer some of her warmth. Instead, she felt cold seeping through flesh and bone. The feeling almost broke her.

"Alice—"

Alice gasped and shrugged off Tess's embrace. She'd seen the old, matted teddy bear pointing the way home. Alice scooped him up and hugged him, his red ribbon a streak of blood against her white neck. "Someone must have lost him. Isn't he lovely?"

Dirty and dejected, the old bear winked at Tess. "He's beautiful."

For a moment, Alice looked troubled. "Do you think it's okay to keep him? What if somewhere there's a lost little girl looking for him?"

Tess smiled. "I think he's been lying lonely for a long time. Why don't you give him a name?"

"Samuel!"

Alice lifted the bear high and spun him around, the joy on her face driving the splinter of despair deeper inside Tess. She turned away, scanning the grey and glimpsed a shining peak. She'd walk free and find Teddy. See him somehow. Meanwhile, Alice would stay lost. Helpless and without hope.

"Come with me. I could lead you out of this place." Even as she spoke, Tess knew it was impossible. Alice had tried before, perhaps with Mary. Sideways was her ever after.

Alice squinted into the grey. "What can you see?"

Tess saw more shining specks. Then, from the corner of her eye, bright yellow bedroom curtains. The whole house wobbled into view, veiled still, but real. The more she stared, the more detail appeared.

"I see a small gate swinging open and beyond that, an orange ball and a green can."

"It's all grey to me. I could walk and walk and never get there. I'm not like you or Mary. My Sideways is all around me, the only thing that's real, but now I have Samuel to keep me company until you come back."

Inside Tess's chest, the clock ticked too fast. Returning wouldn't be easy. She didn't like how Sideways *felt*. Slimy. Like standing in the middle of a dank swamp. She recalled the grey stew and floating meat monsters, stomach lurching.

"I'll wait here for you."

Tess stumbled away. She didn't want to look back but did. Twice, and twice Alice was still there. Watching. Waving.

The rest of the journey home was like waking from a deep, dream-filled sleep. Disorientating, clarity slow, as thick fog inside Tess's head dispersed. She stood inside the gate staring at the orange ball and green can, amazed at their colour. The grey of Sideways had consumed her and now everything looked strange. Felt stranger. She should be running, panicking, screaming for Teddy, but was calm. She went in through the back door and listened to the silence.

"Grandad?"

Inside the shop, Tess felt safe, familiar, inhaling, and relishing the old, musty smell. Several working clocks told her it was 10:49am. She pictured the antique ship's clock in the galley kitchen. As she'd ventured Sideways, it read 10:31, but she'd been gone a long time. Hours, not minutes. *Did that mean a whole day had passed?*

Like balm, Mary's words echoed in her mind. *No time has passed.* So, it was still Sunday morning, which meant Grandad was at church and Teddy wasn't long lost.

Tess had an overwhelming desire to curl up in her blue chair and forget. She touched the soft fabric. On the table sat the book she'd been reading—*The Excruciating History of Dentistry*—and an old silver watch Grandad gave her. 'It's very old and works with the quartz oscillator,' he told her.

Tess put the watch on. It was more like a bracelet, dangling loose. She noticed a bruise on the bone of her wrist and imagined she was nothing but yellowing bone, that she wasn't standing in the shop at all, but had disappeared Sideways. She'd walk through the shop, leaving no trace, no sound.

She ascended the narrow stairs. Stairs she'd climbed hundreds of times, but never with such dread. She'd always thought the brown carpet had swirls, but the pattern had turned into malformed faces with sinister eyes and cruel mouths. Near the top, a stair creaked as it always did.

"Teddy?" Tess felt as though the silence might swallow her. She was drawn to the kitchen window, the little yellow curtains framing her view into the nothing of Sideways. Now she knew it was there, Tess couldn't believe she hadn't seen it before. A desolate wasteland, a grey sea surging, lapping hungrily at the back gate. The bleakness made her shiver. If she had to dive back in with Teddy, she feared they'd both drown. Icy fear crept and sat upon her shoulder. A macabre goblin, tormenting with cruel whispers. She wished Grandad was there, with comforting arms and reassuring words, telling her everything would be okay, but she was alone with only the demon on her shoulder.

Tess turned her back on the window and drank a glass of water. Her hand trembled. She felt the same scratch of broken glass against her lip and tasted blood. She looked at the clock. Time marched on. Already 10:57.

She crept to the bedroom and gazed around, touching the covers of Teddy's empty bed. The room felt lifeless, the sheets cold. She fought back tears, struggling not to dissolve into weeping despair. She puffed up Teddy's pillow. Great-grandad's war medal peeped out. Teddy had been sleeping on it. Tess traced the shape of the medal, then turned it over and read the inscription. For Gallantry. Charles Thomas Smith, Lieutenant. The date read 7th July 1917. Any other time, Tess would've marvelled at the medal, knowing it was her great-grandad's and what it represented. Defeated, she tucked it away in a pocket and sank down upon her unmade bed.

Tess sucked her lip, still tasting blood. She closed her eyes. What use was looking if she couldn't see? Her breath caught as air shifted around her. Definite movement. "I know you're there, Teddy, and know you're scared. I'm scared too, but I'm going to help you, so please, *please*, be brave and do what I tell you."

She imagined Teddy's scrawny arms wrapped around her neck and felt the heat of tears. Her brother was there. She sensed him. Smelled him.

"We have to go back there, okay?"

A wave of terror broke over Tess. Teddy wanted to stay hidden and safe. Perhaps he believed it was a dream, a nightmare from which he'd wake up. In an instant, Tess knew he would flee, and she'd lose him forever. She jumped up, blocking the door, staring into the empty room.

"Please, Teddy. Wait! You must trust me, and I *promise*, I won't let her get you, but you must do as I say. If you try to find Mum, you won't ever come back, and I'll never see you again. Do you understand?"

Tess listened to the stillness over the roaring in her head and sensed panic subside. Teddy trusted her. "Follow closely. I'll protect you."

At the top of the stairs, Tess stopped. The carpet goblin laughed, the one on her shoulder laughed too. Something was wrong. She could smell it. She wanted to retreat to the bedroom and hide under the bedclothes, but Teddy was relying on her, and instinct told her to keep going. Hiding wouldn't save Teddy, neither would giving into fear. His time was running out. Peering down the stairs into the gloom, Tess knew something was there, waiting. She dragged in a shaking breath and trod on the top step. The creak sounded like a door slowly opening, or a lid lifting.

"Grandad," she whispered, reaching the bottom of the stairs. Her heart raced. Dread consumed.

The shop had a visitor. A nightmare vision hunched and grotesque at Grandad's desk. Unmoving, save for the tapping of one finger, keeping perfect time with Tess's heart. Above this abomination, a crown of dust clouds swirled, as though each speck were desperate not to settle.

The Sideways Lady had followed Tess home.

14

Clay and Crown

From a mask of grey clay, two black dots glowered. Eyes with nothing in them. Little black beetle shells. No lines on the face, nor marks of any kind. No eyebrows or lashes. Expressionless. Any hair on the head hidden under the stinking cowl.

Slowly, the creature turned to face Tess. Caught in the beam of sunlight through an opening in the blinds illuminating her crown of spinning dust, ill-fitting flesh looked shiny. Wet clay stretched, hanging loose. When Teddy glimpsed her from the kitchen window, he thought she looked dead, but this was worse. A half-melted wax model come alive.

"Thank you for leading me here." The voice was cold. Like an echo from a deep well.

The Sideways Lady gurgled a laugh. The decaying stench of her breath swept towards Tess. Wrapping around her, ice against her flesh, stinging her eyes. Tess tried to focus on the sound of ticking, but she couldn't hear it over blood thundering through her veins.

"Be brave, Teddy," Tess whispered, but it was hopeless. What chance did she have with this presence in their home?

"That's right, Teddy. Be brave," the creature mocked.

Feeling Teddy's terror somehow lessened Tess's fear. "Stay close, Ted."

"I like it here. I might stay. All these shiny treasures." The Sideways Lady placed her hands on the table. Not proper hands, but shapeless slabs, formed without their creator knowing hands had bones and veins and fingernails.

Tess knew she had to act, but like the dust, her mind swirled. She waited and watched. The visitor seemed in no rush.

"The magic of time. All mine."

Tess was trapped. Half in terror. Half in fascination.

The Sideways Lady leaned over the table, inhaling deeply, as though the scattered treasures gave off a sweet perfume. She licked green-tinged lips, her tongue a slab of stale meat. Her mouth stretched wide, doughy flesh flopping loose. Grotesque hands scooped up the contents of Grandad's table. Tess watched pieces of precious clocks and watches disappear, wincing at the sound of teeth grinding on metal turning everything to dust. With a premonition of that terrible mouth sucking her in, Tess knew she had to move.

"Teddy! Follow me and don't look back."

Tess made a dash for the small kitchen. The back door was open and beyond that, the gate swung wide, beckoning her. Suddenly, Sideways seemed the safest place to be.

15

Hide and Seek

The little mounds of Tess's treasure trail had flattened. She imagined the Sideways Lady swiping them. Gleeful. A spoilt, greedy child. No, not a child. A child's nightmare. The monster from under the bed. The worst of imagination come alive.

Tess fled, understanding her life was now entwined with her tormentor. Instead of the reassuring tick of a clock, her pounding heart sounded and felt like a death chime. She focused on the strewn clock parts, but the terrible image of the Sideways Lady filled her mind. Watching with black eyes. Laughing with gruesome mouth gaping wide.

Sideways bulged with eerie silence and something else. Unseen, but felt. *Could it be other lost souls, all trapped in their own hell? How many children?* Tess swallowed a sob. Couldn't bear to think of Teddy joining their ghostly ranks. She gritted her teeth, driving out the thought.

"Not far now." Tess slowed to a walk, scanning Sideways, certain she was being watched. That the Monster of the Swamp toyed with her. Waiting to ingest them both.

Grandad's gate seemed far away, wobbling in Tess's vision like it may vanish altogether. She couldn't bear being stuck here forever, and Grandad was in danger, too. Apparently, the Sideways Lady liked to make house calls now. In despair, Tess realised in leaving a trail, the rules had changed. She cursed, then winced, knowing Teddy would have heard. If they got home, Teddy would tell on her or repeat it, and she'd be in trouble.

If they got home.

Tess quashed fear twisting her in knots. Ignored the torment in her mind. She had to believe she could save them both.

"You okay, Ted?" She made her voice sound natural, calm.

Ahead, Alice waited. A little girl as grey as her surroundings. Dull hair coiled over her shoulders like thin, fraying rope. Eyes, big empty pools of nothing. Lifeless. Hopeless. A reflection of the battered bear.

Spindly arms wrapped around Tess. "I thought she might gobble you up."

Tess tugged free. "Still here."

Alice kissed her matted bear, a shy smile in place and something else.

Perhaps I'm wrong. Wasn't there a glimmer in the depths of Alice's eyes? A part of her soul surviving, despite everything? Teddy would survive, too. *And they'd all live happily ever after.*

"Let's find my brother."

"He's here somewhere." Alice shielded her eyes and surveyed the land, the way a sailor surveys the sea.

"How can you tell?"

"When the body gets close to its soul, the air fizzes. I can feel it."

Tess closed her eyes. No fizzing, but the creeping sensation of being watched still, and the damp of Sideways making her flesh moist. The flat landscape kept its secrets hidden, including Teddy. With every impossible second that passed, Tess knew she was losing him. "Where is he?" she cried, panic threatening to erupt.

"Is he good at hide and seek?" Alice asked.

A pang of sorrow hit Tess as a bittersweet memory surfaced. "No. He's terrible. He crouches into a ball, hides his face, and thinks we can't see him."

"Then we just need to look past the emptiness. Things disappear out here but come back again when you don't expect them to. I lost my pea-shooter for the longest time, then found it one day, right near the asylum."

The smell worsened, swirling with the Sideways stew. "I think she's coming," Alice hissed, glancing towards the distant glow of Mary's fire.

"Go back. I'll find Teddy."

Alice clenched her fists. "She can't do anymore to hurt me. I'm all used up."

Not my fight. Tess turned away from the pitiful child, gulping down sorrow and guilt. The morbid wind churned around them, stirring up the grey, stirring up the stench. Guided by instinct, Tess crouched down. She pictured Teddy and how he'd be hiding. Hunkered, gangly arms covering his head. Like that, he'd think he was hidden and safe, but he was far from safe. They both were.

Tess controlled her breathing, letting her eyes unpick the grey. Sometimes, when helping Grandad, she used his loupe to see into the tiniest space needing the smallest of screws. For the longest time, she'd never had a watchmaker's eye, couldn't see what Grandad saw, but over time she'd learned to use her eyes for half the job and allow instinct to do the rest.

"There!" Tess pointed, choking as fat tears slid down her cheeks and smeared dirt.

Teddy remained motionless and when Tess touched him, she felt the cold of his flesh through the thin fabric of his pyjamas.

"He needs to get back in his body," Alice said.

"Did you hear that, Teddy? You have to climb back inside yourself."

The hunkered shape remained still.

"He's scared in case he sees her again. If he opens his eyes, she's real, but hiding doesn't work."

"It happened to you …"

Alice nodded, chest heaving with the memory. "Don't let it happen to him."

Tess reached into her pocket and withdrew the medal she'd found under Teddy's pillow. She crouched down next to his body and tucked it in a pocket.

"Did you see that, Teddy? That medal is yours, but you can only have it if you're really brave. Can you be brave?"

Nothing happened. Then, like dry leaves whipped by a wind, the sound of rustling. A noise coming from inside the frozen boy. Bony shoulders quivered.

Teddy was back and threw himself on Tess, trembling in her arms. She cradled him, stroking his head as Mum would. "Shh. You're safe now," she muttered.

In that moment, Tess believed it was so. She'd been desperately afraid but confronted her fear and won. She squeezed her eyes, dispelling an image of the mocking creature, its insidious mouth stretched wide.

"I have something for you." Tess untangled Teddy from her arms and removed her watch. She offered it to Alice. "Take it."

"I've never seen anything so beautiful."

"It means you can see the time passing. I promise, Alice, every time I look at a clock or watch, I'll think of you and do whatever I can to help. Somehow, one day …" Tess cringed, closing her mouth and swallowed the barbed-edged guilt. *What could she do to help Alice?*

Alice traced delicate fingertips over the exquisite watch face. She beamed and her features transformed, light chasing away the pallid hue of her cheeks. For a moment, hell receded, and she looked like a normal little girl.

In the gloomy twilight, something changed.

The grey stirred, a voice coming from nowhere and everywhere. *"How touching."* The Sideways Lady uncurled, from where she'd been hiding in the dirt. Just as Teddy had been. "I'm good at hiding too," she sneered.

Alice turned to Tess, terror in her eyes, the watch forgotten. She stumbled backwards. "Whatever you do, don't close your eyes!" She fled, white hair streaming behind.

The creature wasn't interested in Alice, but if Tess ran, dragging Teddy, the chase would be swift. Clutching each other's hands, brother and sister shrank as the monster loomed, flashing discoloured teeth that reminded Tess of discarded cherry stones.

A big, misshapen head moved from side to side and studied Tess. Tess stared back, horrified at the boneless, bloodless face blotting out everything else. She couldn't blink or swallow. Could barely breathe. She hadn't saved Teddy, but at least he wouldn't die alone. The thought gave her little solace.

In her mind, Mary appeared, distracting her. The old woman said the Sideways Lady was a chaotic creation of trapped, tortured souls. Remains of the angry. The mad. The vengeful. Dangerous eyes flashed, but Tess grasped at reason. Didn't it mean she must also be made up of pain? Confusion? Desperation? Did Tess see that reflected in those malevolent eyes, too?

Something happened between them. A miniscule, surprising shift. Her tormentor saw Tess wasn't trembling with fear, nor weeping in supplication. She'd grown accustomed to children who groped blindly until they turned to dust, or she devoured them. A cruel smile split her face, her caustic stench wafting over Tess in terrible waves. Beetle-black eyes roved hungrily. "You are an interesting specimen."

Tess stepped back. "We're going home."

"How disappointing. I'd like you to stay."

Tess's fingers dug into the flesh of Teddy's arms. "You can't have my brother."

Amused, the creature leered. "And who is going to stop me?"

As Tess prepared herself for the end, a shrill wail pierced Sideways, and a shape emerged from its depths. Withered and small, Mary stood in front of Tess. In her steady hand, a blue flame danced with eerie intent. Snarling, the Sideways Lady recoiled, waxen face rippling as she blanched.

"You'll not keep anyone today," Mary barked.

"You have no dominion over me, hag!"

The spitting flame leapt in Mary's hand and the beast gathered her cloaks about her, snapping and snarling like a rabid dog. A stooped, withered old crone had foiled evil with nothing more than a magic flame.

As the Sideways Lady retreated, black eyes sought Tess, the soulless smile back in place. "Scurry home, little pet, and take the pitiful boy with you. My fun can wait."

Like the flame she held, Mary's eyes blazed. She glanced at Tess. "Take the boy and leave. Now!"

Tess turned, dragging Teddy with her. This time, she never looked back. Through the unchanging gloom, they fled. Free from unspeakable torture, but for how long? The little clock shop, a beacon in the bleak landscape, may no longer be a refuge. She'd invited danger in. Unseen horrors would forever hide in dusty corners. Tess peered at Teddy. He looked too much like Alice—pale and lost—but his flesh felt warm in her hand, and she refused to accept his soul was broken. That he might live only half a life.

Haunted blue eyes darted about. Would he ever fully emerge from his nightmare? Tess squeezed the little hand in hers. "We're safe, Teddy. You don't have to see her again."

"Promise?"

Tess had to believe it possible. The Mistress of Sideways had no power over their lives. She would soon forget the two children who escaped her bleak realm. *Wouldn't she?*

"I promise," Tess said, but the grey swallowed her voice.

16

Demon

With shaking fingers, Tess locked the gate. She'd look for a padlock tomorrow, then throw away the key. Build a barricade if she had to. "Don't go back out there," she said, unsure if Teddy understood.

She held his warm hand, and they stumbled up the steps and through the back door. Another lock. Tess fought with a heavy bolt. It was rusting and stiff, pinching her finger, making her cry out. She watched her finger turn purple and quashed a tide of fury threatening to overcome her.

Beyond the ancient kitchen, all stone and ill-fitting cabinets, the shop embraced them, but it felt different. As though beneath the surface, masked by the clamour of clocks, unease rippled. Her head a muddle, Tess struggled to find words to restore peace.

"Thank you for finding me."

The voice sounded like Teddy. A broken, unfixable version. Tess chewed her lip to stop from crying out. *Was he lost forever?* She plopped down into her chair and Teddy crawled onto her lap and fell asleep. The clock above the shop door read 11:07. Tess closed her eyes. When she opened them, it was 12:09. Still in his coat, Grandad peered down. He went to speak, but something in Tess's face stopped him. Uncomfortable, she stirred, and Teddy woke up.

"Shall I make you a sandwich, Ted?"

Damp with sweat, Teddy nodded and slid from Tess's lap. Four years old again, he stood waiting for her.

"What happened?" Grandad's voice was hushed as if he were still in church. He glanced around the shop, troubled eyes lingering on the empty table. "Shall I put the kettle on?"

Grandad was unyielding in his belief that there was nothing a cup of tea couldn't fix, but Tess had a feeling tea would be next to useless.

"I'll make Teddy's lunch first."

The thought of food repulsed Tess, but she was glad Teddy wanted to eat. She just wished he wasn't sitting in shrunken silence, one hand holding the sandwich, the other clutching the war medal. She fixed her eyes on him, relieved when colour returned to his cheeks. When only crumbs sat on his plate, Tess suggested a nap. She didn't know what else to do. What was the point in probing him, forcing him to relive his terrifying ordeal?

Teddy hadn't had an afternoon nap since he was five, but he allowed Tess to lead him to bed and tuck him in. Without giving it any thought, she leaned down to kiss his forehead, something she'd never done. Teddy's matchstick arms hugged her. Her tears slid into his damp hair. He was fast asleep in minutes.

Tess plodded downstairs. Grandad sat at his empty table watching the drifting dust. The blinds were still down and the light out, creating a gloomier than usual atmosphere. Even the clocks tick-tocked in sombre fashion. The noise and lack of light felt oppressive, unnatural. Tess flicked a switch, bathing the shop's clutter in a dull glow. It did little to dispel the gloom. She approached the empty table, then faltered. The lines on Grandad's face looked deeper. He appeared older, frail. A trick of the light, Tess told herself. Shadows making him look ancient and giving a haunted expression.

Wearily, Tess perched on the stool, feeling his gaze upon her, but she didn't know what to say, or where to start. Silence ebbed and flowed with the ticking clocks, a familiar feeling of peace settling. It was short-lived.

A strangled sound startled her. Finally, she looked into Grandad's tortured eyes. He'd been crying, or perhaps it was the dust. Despite the efforts of a weekly cleaner, dust clung to every book and clock—unless it swirled above the head of the Sideways Lady.

Grandad retrieved a handkerchief and dabbed his eyes, composing himself. He placed a hand on the table, the tremble unmistakable. "What happened?"

Tess's spluttered words were jumbled. "I came downstairs, and she was sitting there, and swallowed it all. Ate everything on your desk. *She just ate it.* Was the princess's clock there? What will you say? I'm sorry, Grandad."

He opened a hidden drawer and held out a treasure trove of watch and clock components. "I've made and fixed watches and clocks for many years, as did my father and grandfather before me. We'd be out of business if we left anything of value sitting on top of our workstation."

Tess slumped in relief. "Of course, the secret drawer."

When she was little, the secret drawer was out of bounds. 'Too many precious things for careless fingers,' she was told. Young Tess struggled to understand why such tantalising treasures were denied until Grandad revealed a different drawer. A trove of magic in which she could immerse herself.

Grandad hid the valuables away and settled his gaze upon Tess. He waited, clutching his hands together as if in prayer. A great weariness stole over her. She wanted nothing more than to curl up and pretend it was all a terrible dream. The old man understood. He sighed and nodded, hiding blue beneath the hoods of his eyes.

"Is Teddy okay?" the gravelled voice asked.

"We'll be home Tuesday. He'll be fine once he's back with Mum."

"And you, Tess? Just tell me you're okay."

Tess stood. "I need sleep, then I'll be fine."

"I should never have left you alone." He folded Tess into his arms.

Tess nestled against his generous paunch, felt the familiar scratch of woollen jumper, and for a moment she felt little again, and protected. She clung to the feeling, as she clung to him, but behind closed eyes she saw *her.* Grandad couldn't protect her. No one could.

The bed was cold, but Tess snuggled deep. Across the room, Teddy's gentle breathing soothed. She thought she may have trouble sleeping, but drifted off easily, sailing into the dark where there was nothing. Woken by screams, she bolted upright, heart driving hard against her chest. Teddy whimpered, madly staring about. Before Tess could unscramble from her covers, Grandad was there. He tugged Teddy towards him and wrapped him in protective arms.

"Shh," he whispered again and again, stroking Teddy's hair, trying to calm him. "Just a dream. Safe here." He looked up at Tess and their eyes locked. Even through the mottled gloom of dusk, Tess knew he no more believed it than she did.

Teddy went back to sleep far quicker than Tess expected, but frayed nerves stopped her lying down again. Lured by the smell of cheese on toast, she padded through to the kitchen, smiling wanly as she flopped into a chair.

"So, is there a plan?" Grandad put a plate in front of Tess.

Hungrily, she breathed in the smell, but felt unsettled still. It occurred to her she might be sick, but perhaps lack of food was the reason. She picked up a slice of greasy toast and tore off an edge. "No sausages?"

Grandad smirked and sat down with his own supper. "Not tonight. Well? Plan?"

Tess shrugged. "Get Teddy home, and hope. What else can I do?"

Water dripped from the tap. Like someone tapping a finger. Grandad toyed with his supper. "As a boy, I was warned not to go Sideways. Stories had passed down, and it scared me to venture out there. But then, boys, you know. Despite the warnings, I was intrigued and invincible. I thought I was clever. Not so clever as it turned out. Just lucky."

"What happened?"

"It was a long time ago, but afterwards, I lay awake at night, thinking of that smell and how there was something inside the grey waiting to jump out at me."

What had Mary called Tess? Wilful and heedful. Most people couldn't smell Sideways at first, but she was different. "You can smell it, too?"

"Every time, yes."

"Did you always want to be a clockmaker?"

"Since I was knee-high to a grasshopper."

Tess thought of Teddy, his pale skin, the haunted expression in his eyes. He was too young to know who he was. Most children were. If Mary was right, and that was the only weapon against Sideways, they were all doomed. She toyed with the remains of her toast, thick, greasy cheese slumping from the edge of the bread. It reminded Tess of *her* face. Loose, misshapen. No skeleton. She pushed the plate away.

"We'll be safe at home." Tess pictured the semi-detached house where she lived. The opulent garden and pond filled with fish. The tree-lined street with big, shiny cars, polite neighbours, and their elegant cats, but there was the dark alley leading from the row of local shops to the main road beyond. A forbidden, stinking artery. And what of the murky waters of the canal? The abandoned scout hut daubed with graffiti, or the bleak field beyond growing discarded cans and crisp packets?

It didn't mean any of it was Sideways, Tess told herself. She'd never given Sideways a thought before and neither had Teddy, but she remembered *her* warning and a terrible feeling of dread settled inside.

Tess went to bed and watched Teddy sleep. It wasn't fully dark, and she could see his pale face in the gloom. She imagined his complexion paler than usual, or perhaps it was the moon casting beams through gaps in the lightweight curtain. Tess continued to watch until she could no longer make out Teddy's features in the dark. Then she closed her eyes and let the monsters made of night chase away the Sideways Lady. She always came back.

Tess was in the little room at Grandad's. The black, total. The silence, simmering. Something was in the room with her. *She had to be dreaming.* Less than a metre away, Teddy slept. Tess could make out his outline. She wanted to cry out but had no voice. She tried to move but was paralysed. A shape bulged before her tortured eyes. *A demon hiding in the dark.*

She struggled against invisible binds holding her rigid in bed, then sudden release. Tess scrambled upright, hugging her knees, holding back her scream. Her eyes shut tight, and she waited for her heart to return to the steady sound of a ticking clock. When they opened, the monster had gone.

Shivering, Tess climbed out of bed and padded to Grandad's bedroom. The door stood ajar. She nudged it open, willing him to be awake so she could hear his voice, but low snores came from the dark patch on the bed. She retreated and crept towards the bathroom, grasping the wall for support. A sudden noise jolted her. She peered downstairs. Familiar shapes outlined in the gloom. No monsters. The desk was still a desk. Clocks, still clocks.

Tess heard the noise again. The creak of a chair. A smell drifted towards her and sweat slimed across her body. The Sideways Lady had returned, wanting to claim her pet.

17

A Flea-ridden Gift

Someone snarled Tess's name, then movement. A ghostly face with staring eyes. Tess slumped against the wall. She wanted to weep. "Mary. What are you doing here?"

"No need to wake anyone else," a voice barked.

Tess grabbed her jumper and stole downstairs. At first, she couldn't see Mary, but there she was, snuggled in Tess's blue chair, eyes flashing in amusement.

Mary grinned with teeth that looked like pieces of charred onion. "Sit."

Tess resisted the urge to ask her to move and pulled up a stool. "How did you get here?"

"*How did I get here?* I walked."

Tess didn't know if the old woman was mocking her and pulled a face. Why did she feel insignificant in the presence of this ancient creature? "What I meant was, how did you get in?"

The unmistakable glint in Mary's eyes implied Tess ought to know.

"I locked the doors." Tess waved her finger, showing off the purple splodge.

"Yet here I am."

"So you can walk through doors?"

Mary chuckled. A deep, throaty sound. "You 'ave far too much imagination. As soon as I step from Sideways, I have access to *my* London. No doors are locked to me."

"I see." Tess wasn't sure she did see. She crossed, then uncrossed her leg.

Mary stared, waiting for the next question.

"Your London. So, not the same time, but the same place and unchanged."

A withered hand stroked the pages of an open book. "More or less."

"And different people?"

The glint was back in Mary's eyes. Definitely mocking.

"Of course, different people. Silly me."

"Your ancestors have always made me welcome."

Tess wondered if she should offer tea. Instead, she said, "Why are you here?"

"You knows why." Mary chomped at her lips with two rotten teeth.

"I've no idea. How's Alice?"

"You knows that too."

Tess glowered. "It's late, Mary. Either tell me why you're here or leave."

Mary arched wiry eyebrows. Her eyes blazed. "Sit."

Tess hovered, then sat, running fingers through hair she hadn't washed in days. "I just want to take Teddy home so he can forget about this. No child should have to go through what he's been through."

"Quite right."

Alice. "I mean, I know Alice has been through a lot …"

Mary sniffed and chomped.

Tess squirmed. "You can't blame me for looking out for my brother." Even as she said the words, Tess knew it was far from being that simple.

Mary graced Tess with a withering look. "I'm 'ere to talk about you, not 'im."

"We're going home. Mum will pick us up tomorrow and this can all be forgotten."

"D'you think you can forget, then? D'you think *she* will let you forget?"

Tess noticed a bug scurrying along the track of blue veins on Mary's wrinkled hand. It disappeared inside the folds of her sleeve, and it occurred to Tess that the old woman was secured by her great many layers. Glued together with dirt.

Mary crossed swollen ankles and squinted with disapproval. "I never needed to know much about anything, but I always knew about Sideways. Ever since *she* got waked, I've known about 'er and you should know, too."

"Know what?"

"She don't like being stuck there alone, and she likes you."

"Lucky me."

"I can sense 'er desire and it's *powerful*. I'll warrant you'll not sleep like you used to."

"Can she ... is she able to get inside my mind?"

Clocks ticked, and Mary inclined her head. "Sideways were quiet tonight," she mumbled.

There *had* been something in the dark pinning Tess to the bed. Impossible to pretend it was just a dream. *Mary saw.*

Mary clutched the arms of the chair. "Did she pay you a visit?"

Tess's silence was answer enough.

"Well, then ..."

Hopefully, Tess waited, but Mary focused on the ceiling, filling the space with her presence and stink. Tess was getting used to the smell—if she didn't get too close to the old woman—but there was so much more to the bag of rags and bone sitting in her favourite blue chair. Understanding unravelled and stretched. Mary was a gift. A dirty, flea-ridden gift.

"That wasn't real, was it? The fire in your hand?"

Mary's smile had a hint of pride. "She don't need to know it weren't. I've always had magic and a fair few years to refine my skills."

"Thank you," Tess mumbled.

Mary lifted a crooked finger, dark with dirt. "You promised Alice you'd help, and you gave 'er that watch. Why? What use is it if you don't intend coming back? Poor child has nonsense in 'er head and looking out for you every second."

Tess jumped up, feeling inadequate in the face of Mary's ferocious gaze. "I don't know what to do. How can you expect me to help? I'm fifteen!"

With surprising ease, Mary rose, too. She glanced around the shop. "This place is 'ere for a reason and 'ere you are. Capable. Defiant. Question is, are you brave enough to face the creature, or will you close your eyes and pretend it's not real?"

"I'm not brave enough."

"Then why'd you make Alice believe you are? All that nonsense with the watch, making promises you can't keep! Poor child's turning to dust before my eyes, but now she believes you can save 'er."

Tess peered through the slats of the blind, the grey light of dawn upon the street. Some way distant, there was a crash. Something heavy. A man's shout. The market. London coming to life, despite the early hour.

Mary was by Tess's side. "You do what you think is right, but may be worth remembering, the littlun's not like you and Sideways is in 'im."

"But he'll forget, won't he? Or think it was just a dream?"

Mary shrugged. "Might be lucky."

"What does that mean?"

The old woman whistled down her big nose. "Look, he has a chance. I'm not saying that, but Sideways weakens your mind and spirit, and over time—"

"Over time, what?"

Mary clawed at her rags, drawing them closer. "I doubt 'e'll ever be truly free, but neither will you now." A flicker of pity flashed in Mary's eyes, but she blinked it away. "Took me a long time to get 'ere. Need to get back to me fire."

"Wait a minute. You're like me, you said. Why haven't you ever done anything?"

"Impossible for me."

"Not good enough, Mary."

Mary fidgeted inside her rags. "I come from another time. Never went to school or got any 'tificates, but I know what I knows and this shop, the people in it—*you*—can stop 'er." She hobbled away, a hunched figure cocooned in rags and dirt.

Her imprint and odour lingered. Tess took a breath. "Would you like a bath before you go?"

Mary limped back, milky eyes roving across Tess's face, then she pulled her stinking blanket tighter. "Like them boots you wear, my dirt is a barrier against the world, but sometimes, my girl, you need to let your guard down. It's too late for me. I'm old. I wouldn't be me without me dirt, but you're still you, even without those ugly boots."

Tess wiggled bare feet. "I'm not wearing my boots."

Through the grime on Mary's face, Tess glimpsed contempt, but the old woman said no more. She didn't need to. Despite the raging injustice, the truth, ice cold in the pit of Tess's stomach, was impossible to deny. She watched Mary trail through the kitchen and back Sideways.

Back inside the shop, Tess gazed around, trying to ignore the lurking shadows. She'd never been afraid of the dark or monsters hiding under the bed, but now the corners hid goblins, and the monster was real. With sudden vehemence, Tess jabbed the light switch. "*Not me. Not my fight.*"

Unafraid of the light, the beasts followed her as she climbed the stairs.

18

Entices the Child

Tess snuggled into lumpy covers, but cold sat in her bones. In the gloom, she squinted at Teddy, relieved that at least he could sleep. In the morning, he'd think it was all a dream. Forget the horror he endured. *Would she?* She burrowed deeper, hiding in the dark. Despite torturous thoughts, heavy eyelids closed, and she slept.

Light sneaking through the thin curtains woke Tess, the brightness and peace of the morning at odds with the chaos in her mind. But she'd fought battles there before and won.

Teddy's bed was empty. The ancient alarm clock read 7:15. She could hear the shower at full blast. Grandad. Teddy wouldn't shower without being bribed. Tess didn't want to feel afraid, but the air was icy, and a creeping sensation chilled her more. She should never have fallen asleep! With spiralling dread, she reached out to the curtains and yanked them apart.

The gate was ajar. Beyond, in the shallow of the merciless ocean, Teddy stood transfixed. Tess banged on the window. It would be okay. Unmoving, Teddy was in plain sight. She shouted his name and banged again, hurting her knuckles. It was useless trying to open the window. White gloss paint had sealed it many years before.

Please, Teddy. Turn around.

Downstairs was far away, and Tess didn't want to let Teddy out of her sight. She couldn't lose him again, but Grandad wouldn't hear her cries over the shower. She must dash. Barefoot, she ran from her room and hurtled down the stairs two at a time. Taking the corner into the kitchen too tight, she crashed against the doorframe but didn't care. The back door stood open, affording her a view of the courtyard and beyond. *Where was he?*

Tess jumped the two steps and flew through the gate. The stench of Sideways slammed into her. There! He'd waded deeper but turned to greet her. Tess blanched at the strange smile on his face.

"Come inside," she choked.

Teddy pointed, blue eyes shining. "A silver river."

Tess looked down. Perhaps Teddy saw the glint of ruined peaks, but the undulating grey had long since swallowed the treasures. The earth was barren. "There is no silver, Ted."

But Teddy didn't hear. Oblivious to the smell, convinced of what he saw, he tottered deeper into the swell. Tess made to grab him, but red-faced and fierce, the little boy struggled. "I have to follow it."

Tess kept hold, fear lending strength. "You're still in pyjamas. Let's go inside and get dressed. Perhaps I can come. Later."

Teddy gazed out with longing, the fixed smile still in place. "Promise?"

How had it come to this? How had he forgotten his terror from the day before? Tess crouched low and clutched his twig arms. She'd fallen asleep last night believing it best if Teddy thought Sideways a dream, but she was wrong. He *must* remember what it meant to be swallowed out there. He must remember his fear. *Her face.*

"Don't you remember being lost and afraid?" Tess felt his flesh beneath grasping fingers, but Teddy's face remained a smiling mask. She had the horrible sensation he couldn't see her, that all he could see from the corner of his eye was the promise of something shiny and new. If she let go, he'd disappear. Lost forever. She held tight.

"Don't you remember *her*? The Sideways Lady?"

The gate banged and startled them both.

"Tess. Teddy. Mum's on the phone." Concern marked Grandad's face. He frowned at Tess, but the spell had broken.

Teddy dashed inside. "Me first," he called.

Tess followed on shaking legs, smiling weakly. "Need to buy a padlock, Grandad."

19

Shadows and Dreams

Home. A strange place for Tess. Over her shoulder, goblins laughed in sinister clouds and Smelly Mary was never far from her thoughts, clomping around wafting filthy rags, narrowed eyes accusing.

Though frustrating, Ivor's monotonous honeymoon pictures were a distraction.

"We saw lots of dolphins all around the boat. Look there!"

Tess spied several fin tips amid the wash of the boat and grey waves. She stifled a yawn and snuck a glance at Mum. Even she looked exhausted.

"It was spectacular. Wasn't it, Jodie?"

"It was a lovely honeymoon." Jodie patted Ivor's hand.

Tess smiled at her stepdad. From awkward new boyfriend to bumbling father figure, Ivor failed to inspire Tess's respect. The man was dull. Even his voice was flat. The worst thing about him was his staring fisheyes. Tess imagined them popping out and landing with a squelch on his cheek. None of it would matter if he made Mum happy, but in two years, Tess hadn't seen a spark of passion in her fading blue eyes.

After dissecting every picture, Ivor excused himself. Tess sighed, a ghost of a smile upon her face.

"Sorry, love." Jodie's fingers fluttered.

Mum had smoked for many years and Tess often thought the flutter an ingrained desire to hold a cigarette.

"I'm glad you had a nice time."

"We did. Thank you for looking after Teddy."

The words jolted, and a surge of adrenalin spiked Tess's veins. How could she explain what had happened when Mum didn't seem present? When her expression was always so far away?

Jodie heaved herself from the chair and pulled out a frying pan. "Hungry?"

"Sure." Tess closed her eyes, thoughts converging, words forming, then fleeting. In the end, it was impossible to breach the gap with her voice. Instead, she wrapped her arms around Mum's thick waist. In their comfortable corner of London, Sideways didn't exist and Teddy, pale and quiet, would soon forget. They both would. Tess breathed deeply and ushered Mary from her mind.

"Love you, Mum."

"Love you too, darling."

Every morning, Tess flung her curtains wide and rejoiced in the sunlight and accompanying warmth. She read lots and played music. No one would guess the conflict she hid.

Every night, as darkness edged inside her room, Tess saw demon eyes glittering in shadows. When she slept, babbling laughter woke her from troubled dreams, but Tess defied the shadows and denied her dreams. The whispers inside her mind were harder to ignore. Over and over—*The Sideways Lady comes for me*—but she wouldn't give in.

For years, she'd ignored comments about the red, angry scar on her neck, and the pain of Dad's abandonment. Every day, she ignored disappointed glances at her boots and crumpled T-shirts. Tess was skilled at ignoring things.

She turned the music up and bought a pair of sparkly trainers. Eventually, she'd feel normal again. Free. That's what she told herself every day and every day she believed it a little more.

20

Faraway Sky

Near home was a canal Tess enjoyed strolling along. Looking at the boats, dissecting the lives of people living onboard. Two types of people. Those who transformed their narrow homes into a luxury space with polished decks and plush outside seating, and those who ignored creeping decay. Boats mottled with mould. Dirty curtains hanging from grimy windows. Tess walked a little quicker when she passed those boats. On warm days, their aroma spilled onto the canal path.

That balmy, early September day, Tess scurried past putrid boats, ignoring the strange sensation of being watched. A man with greying blond hair and blue eyes behind round glasses caught her attention. A tall, handsome man. Incredulous, Tess stepped closer to the boat. "Dad?"

She glimpsed the man again before he disappeared through the hatch, puzzled and a little hurt by his reaction. Perhaps he hadn't heard her and, though horrible to imagine, hadn't recognised her. It had been a couple of years. *Did Mum know he was here? Perhaps it was a surprise.* Tess laughed, a joyful feeling exploding in her chest.

Questions whizzed through her mind, but a flame of burning excitement was impossible to ignore. She stepped on the first rung of the ladder, gripping rails slick with slime, then edged around the side of the cabin to the hatch in the middle of the boat. It was dark inside and quiet. To keep the surprise intact, Tess guessed Dad was pretending he wasn't there, but she had to see him now.

The catch was slippery and stiff. Tess peered into the gloom of the cabin, heart drumming inside her head. She hesitated, then a face appeared. Well-worn. Loved. "It is you!"

Despite the cloaking dark, Tess was certain she saw a sparkle in Dad's eyes. Before she could speak again, he ducked from sight, hiding in the bowels of the boat. Tess frowned, but her desire to see him overrode any doubt. There would be a perfectly good explanation for the awkwardness. Holding carefully, she descended the tricky stairs. Musty shadows swirled, but he was there, waiting. Tess grinned and stepped towards him, a warm, fuzzy feeling engulfing her.

Why wasn't he smiling or speaking?

"Dad?"

Something was wrong. His smile was wrong, and blue eyes weren't sparkling at all. The man stepped forward, his hand reaching, the strange smile intact.

Wash from a passing vessel made the boat creak and list. The motion soothed and time passed in slow motion. Tess drifted, overcome with the need to feel loving arms about her. She wanted that more than anything. Tears wet her cheeks as she gazed at the open hatch above, glimpsing a faraway sky, a distant bird, then a waft of greasy chips travelling towards her. Normal things but fading. Soon there'd be nothing. The cabin grew dark as phantom shadows gobbled light. Tess allowed her gaze to return to the apparition before her. *Dad, but not Dad.*

Tess was powerless, lost, and then an ancient voice hissed inside her mind.

"Run!"

Tess had never been so grateful for her flea-ridden friend. Spell broken, she scrambled up slippery steps, breathless, fear slowing her. Any moment, fingers would wrap around her ankle and tug her back into the veil of obscurity. Not far away, the sky stretched out calm and blue. Tess gagged at the festering slime of the boat, then slipped on green mould carpeting the hull. She reached out to steady herself, but her feet slid from under her, and she toppled.

Falling was bad enough, hitting icy, dank water a whole lot worse. Frantically, she flapped around, fearful of drowning. Memories of childhood. Slipping away from Dad's outstretched hand before he grabbed her and pulled her to safety. Tess broke through the surface, cold water washing away tears.

Open-mouthed and staring, a boy stood on the bank holding a bag of hot chips. He waved one in her direction, a smirk spreading across his face. "Hi, Tess."

"Hi, Rav." In the heat of embarrassment, Tess forgot about the cold.

"You okay?"

"Peachy."

Rav laughed and reached out to her. As Tess grasped his hand, she tried not to stare into toffee-coloured eyes. Hoisted free of the canal, she shivered, dripping foul water onto the footpath. "Thanks."

"Sure you're okay?"

"I will be once I'm out of these clothes."

The flush returned to Tess's cheeks as Rav studied the growing puddle.

"Chip?"

"No, thanks."

Rav frowned. "What made you go on there?"

Tess wiped a weary hand across her face, smearing tears and scum. She glanced back at the boat. Strung across the railing, a 'No Entry' sign she hadn't seen. The boat was derelict, decorated with black mould, and listing. Plant life grew through cracks and rot had eaten parts of the deck. She shuddered to think what would have happened had the deck collapsed under her weight. "I thought I saw someone I knew."

"On that?"

Tess hugged herself and turned her back on the boat. Uneasy, Rav shuffled.

"Stupid, I know," Tess mumbled.

"Well, when you're dry, maybe next weekend—next Saturday—d'you want to grab some chips?"

"Sure. Yeah."

Rav grinned, and Tess thought she saw a pink blush colour his chocolate skin. The waft of dank canal water embraced them both, but neither noticed.

"You better go and dry." Rav's eyes glowed warmly and for a moment Tess could pretend every bad thing was mere imagination. On the cold walk home, reality doused her bones. None of it had been real. She'd been lured. Not by Sideways as most were, but by the Sideways Lady inside her head. The warm tingle she'd felt standing close to Rav disappeared in the bleak cold of a monster's steady gaze.

Jodie greeted Tess with pursed lips and a glance at the mud-splattered trainers.

"Oh, Tess."

"Sorry," Tess said, dripping dirty water onto the carpet.

Jodie rummaged inside a hall cupboard, draped a towel about Tess's shoulders, and marched to the kitchen. Squelching, Tess followed and flopped into a chair.

"What's going on, Tess?"

"I fell in the canal."

Jodie plonked opposite. "I mean, everything. What's going on with you?"

"What do you mean?"

Tess studied a ring of milk on the table and held her breath, daring to hope Mum knew everything. Until that moment, she hadn't realised ignoring Sideways wasn't working out. Tess glanced up, met Jodie's tired eyes, and couldn't find the words.

"Sorry about my trainers and stupid hair and stupid boots."

Jodie pushed a box of tissues at Tess. "Your trainers can go in the washing machine and as for your hair, it looks lovely sometimes. When it's brushed."

Tess laughed, choking back tears. "And my boots?"

"You wore your trainers today." Jodie smiled, clasping Tess's hand.

"I thought I saw Dad."

"Oh." Jodie withdrew her hand and folded her arms.

Dad wasn't a good topic of conversation, but the cold and stink of the canal soaked through Tess's flesh. She felt tired, unwell, and needed to share her burden. "Mum, what do you know about Sideways?"

21

Urban Legend

Jodie flopped back in her chair, wooden struts protesting. Her eye twitched. "What did Grandad tell you?"

From her pursed lips, narrowed eyes, and fluttering fingers, Tess couldn't fathom whether her mother was angry or afraid. She shrugged, suddenly irritated and reluctant to talk.

"That man! Look, Tess, when he was a boy growing up with the dump behind the shop, it was harmless for Grandad to believe, but nowadays, we know all that stuff isn't real. He had no right to fill your head with nonsense."

"You don't believe in it, then?"

"Certainly not!" Jodie snorted.

Tess pressed on, her voice barely a whisper. "You don't believe in the Sideways Lady, either?"

For a moment, their eyes met, then Jodie looked away. Before she hid her eyes, Tess saw her confusion. The blotched flush of cheeks, frantic fingers fluttering against the battered wooden table. "Mum?"

With a jolt, Jodie glanced up and smiled. An odd smile. Out of place. She tugged at a strand of greying hair. "Once I believed, but none of it's real. *She*'s not real."

Tess saw the spinning halo of dust above a clay face, smelled the terrible perfume. A wave of resentment rose.

Why couldn't Mum *see*? It was her job to protect Tess, not ignore the desperation in her eyes, nor pretend everything was okay. Disappointment tasted bitter and kept the tears away.

"Did you ever explore the dump?" Tess asked coldly.

"Why would I? Horrible place. Smelly and dirty. Besides, I rarely went to the shop."

Tess frowned and went to speak, but Jodie interrupted scraping back her chair. She heaved herself from the table and went to the kettle, turning her back.

"Nothing but urban legend, Tess. Made up stuff to give you nightmares."

The conversation was over.

Tess drummed her fingers in time with the ticking of the clock. It heightened the silence, then she realised the clock hadn't worked for months. Ivor must have put new batteries in. He was good at things like that. She laid her head on her arms.

Jodie bustled, clattering cups, pouring milk. "Are you going to tell me what happened at the canal?"

She tricked me, Mum. She's inside my head and I fell into the canal, escaping.

"I fell in, Mum. Thought I saw Dad and fell in."

"He's still in Denmark. He hates London, remember?"

The ticking was loud. Irritating. Morose Tess nodded.

"Besides, I'd tell you if he came back, wouldn't I?"

Tess lifted her head. The kettle shrieked. "Can we go and see him soon? I think Teddy would like it."

"We'll see."

Tess gazed around the kitchen, hating how shiny everything was, how ordered. Mum's ceramic birds appraised her. She scowled, feeling overwhelmed with the desire to smash them. Ivor's presence was there now, too. His mug and garden boots, sitting neatly by the back door. Tess felt like a stranger.

Her body shivered, dripping stagnant water onto the freshly mopped floor. Snivelling and miserable, she wondered why Mum kept her back to her. She wanted to stamp and scream. *Why can't you see?*

Tess stood. "I'm going to have a shower."

Jodie turned the kettle off, finally turning to face Tess. "Wait, we have news." *We?* The word sounded like betrayal.

Tess collapsed back into the seat as the front door opened, then closed again. Ivor beamed in the kitchen doorway.

"Have you told her yet?"

Tess looked from Ivor to Mum and back again. "Told me what?"

Ivor settled in a chair. "You're wet."

"I'll get dry in a minute."

"Smelly, too."

Tea forgotten, Jodie cleared her throat, twisting a tea towel between her fingers as she sat down again. "She thought she saw Jan."

"Oh." Fisheyes bulged.

Tess hid her smirk. "Are you going to let me in on the secret?"

Recovered, Ivor winked. An irritating wink. Tess knew what was coming and clenched her fists in readiness.

"I'll give you three guesses."

Tess stood. "I'm cold and wet. You can tell me when I come back."

"We're going on holiday."

"Oh."

Ivor glared at Jodie for spoiling the surprise.

Tess glared, too. "You mean all of us?"

Uneasy, Jodie smiled. "The four of us. As a family."

"Where?"

"I'll give you three guesses."

117

Tess fought the urge to swear at her stepdad. Instead, she pasted a smile on her face.

Jodie patted Ivor's hand and Tess noticed how it appeased him. As though he were a forlorn dog seeking constant assurances. *A pet.* She gulped and trembled inside the cocoon of wet towel. "Are you going to tell me where we're going?"

Jodie took a breath. "Wales. We're going to Wales. Of course, Ivor knows it well."

Tess liked Wales. She'd been there a few times.

"Imagine he does, being Welsh."

Ivor was beaming again. "Have you ever been ghyll scrambling?"

Alone in her bedroom, rage built inside Tess. She wanted to throw something. To smash and scream. She picked up a slipper and hurled it, watching the fluffy, wingless bird land with a thunk. She thumped the wall, hurt her fist, then knocked her head with sharp knuckles. Eventually, the desire to scream subsided.

Whether or not she liked it, the trip to Wales was on regardless of the plans she'd made with her friend Amelia; an afternoon of board games would have been perfect. A sleepover, perhaps. They could talk about Rav. *Did she have a date?* Tess flopped on the bed. Whispering voices filled her mind. Mary. Mum's denial that Sideways existed. Her own troubled thoughts. Tess thought she might be going mad.

The mirror above her desk glittered, sunlight bouncing off it and throwing a golden spear across the beige carpet. Maybe a holiday would be good, if not for her, then for Teddy. Get away from London and the canal.

She strode to the mirror. "Sideways does *not* exist," she chanted. Grimacing at her reflection, Tess saw the ghost of Mary and Alice. "No!"

She threw the towel over the mirror. She would not let ghosts dictate her life.

22

Cave of Ghosts

Despite misty drapes covering Wales, Teddy's smile and ice-cream-coated face further emboldened Tess. He'd live a normal life, which meant she could, too. She enjoyed the smug feeling. Mary didn't know everything, after all.

From her little bedroom, overlooking an expanse of hazy hills, Tess relished the quiet and sense of peace. They'd be back home midweek, and she was meeting Rav at the weekend. The week after, back to school. Normal life was resuming. Ghosts absent.

She heard a shriek. *Teddy.*

"I don't want to go without you!"

Tess jumped from her bed, a feeling of dread wiping out the contentment. In the tiny kitchen of their holiday cottage, Jodie winced as she extended her leg. "I can barely move."

Ghyll scrambling had been exhilarating, but physical.

Teddy wrapped himself around Jodie, tears and snot plastering his face. In the end, it was the promise of a morning ice-cream that stopped the tears. Ivor was unimpressed. Tess smirked. Without Mum, the journey was fraught. Teddy grumbled and Ivor played pipe music too loud. Eventually, Ivor steered into a gravel car park. His car was the only one there.

Tess turned to Ivor. "Where are we going?" she asked hopefully.

"Surprise."

I'm not five! "Can't wait."

Rain beat down, heavy drops splashing against their legs. Tess feigned enthusiasm as Ivor pointed out invisible landmarks. Finally, he led them down a path towards a veiled beach, slipping and sliding on the gravel until arriving at a cave mouth.

Rain dripped from Ivor's frizzy hair. "This is not in any brochures. Me and a friend found this one day and agreed to only tell very special people about it. Are you ready for Ivor's magical caving experience?"

"Ready when you are," Tess muttered, keen to get out of the rain.

Teddy turned to Tess, his eyes troubled pools. "I don't want to go in there. What if *she's* there?"

All remaining warmth drained from Tess. She stared into the dark void of the cave and felt the back of her neck prickling. *Had she misheard?* The rain pitter-pattered on Teddy's plastic mac. "What did you say, Ted?"

"Are we ready?" Ivor chirped.

"Ted? You okay?" Tess felt less than okay herself.

"I'm afraid."

"Don't be silly!" Mocking Teddy's fear, Ivor lowered himself, eyes bulging. He poked Teddy's belly. "Ivor will protect you."

Tess reached out. "Hold my hand, Ted."

She tugged, and Teddy tripped after her. Uncaring, Ivor strode ahead, the light on his helmet showing the way and giving life to shadows in the corners.

"It's just a cave, Ted," Tess whispered as they crunched over crumbling rock.

"Are we walking over bones?"

The prickle at the back of Tess's neck curled down her spine as they edged deeper into the cave.

"It's dark," Teddy whimpered.

Tess's voice echoed. "Caves *are* dark. Focus on Ivor's torch. We can't get lost."

Ivor marched ahead, glancing left and right, his torch throwing shapes and shadows around. Then he stopped and turned, blinding them. "This is it!"

Behind him, halfway up the wall of the cave, a crawl space. A dark hole, accessible by natural steps in the rock.

"Follow me."

He climbed the steps, moisture squelching beneath his tread, stones scattering to the ground, echoing. An eerie sound, like heavy drops of water.

Teddy struggled free. "I don't want to."

"Look at Ivor's fat bum. If you hurry, you can poke it and make him pop."

Teddy sniggered, allowing Tess to lead him to the stone steps and lift him to the first one. She watched as he climbed, his yellow mac a blob of light in the gloom. Impatiently, Ivor called out, and Tess gritted her teeth. She'd worked hard, but her efforts were undone. Ivor was an idiot.

The hole in the wall was a narrow passage surrounded by unforgiving stone. Tess avoided thinking bad thoughts, but they came anyway, playing tricks on her. Tunnel walls bulged and faces etched in stone laughed. Rational Tess knew she was safe, but she couldn't shrug off the sensation she was heading into the heart of Sideways. Fear and sweat prickled her scalp, but she focused on Teddy, the dull yellow ahead, the glare of Ivor's torch leading the way.

"Easy peasy. Well done, Ted."

Ivor dropped down, disappearing. The tunnel was shrouded in darkness, but then an amber strobe of light appeared. He called out, "Wait until you see my cave of ghosts!"

Tess wasn't sure if Teddy heard, but he kept on. Panting, plastic mac crackling. At the end, he froze, and Tess squeezed next to him.

The Cave of Ghosts was a small drop from the crawl space. Surrounded by swirling mist, Ivor stood, hands on hips and wearing a jubilant expression. Shining with moisture, an arced ceiling expanded above him and somewhere in the gloom, the steady, sombre sound of dripping. The cave was cold, creepy.

"Drop down. Come on, Ted. I'll catch you," Ivor called.

Teddy whimpered.

"It's okay," Tess said, eyeing the swirling mist in discomfort. The Cave of Ghosts was aptly named.

"Why don't you climb down first, Tess, then Teddy will follow."

"He's frightened, Ivor."

"Don't be silly. I'm here." Ivor held out his arms, his face a bleached mask in the cave's twilight.

Teddy squirmed from the edge, as if trying to hide inside his yellow coat, retreating like a tortoise into its shell. He sniffled.

Ivor made a snatch for him, grabbing hold of his arms. "Got you!"

Teddy screamed and squirmed. Panting, Ivor held fast. "Let me go!"

Teddy wailed. Ivor tugged.

"Push him towards me," Ivor grunted.

"I won't push him. Let him go. You're scaring him."

Tess prised Teddy from Ivor's rigid hold. With the ghosts swirling behind him, Ivor scrambled towards them, knocking his helmet askew. The light stuttered and his face transformed. He was the bogeyman, or something else unworldly, his face slick with sweat. Malformed features glowed white. There was madness in his popped eyes.

Tess looked away. *Just Ivor.* Her mind churned, dulling her senses and shutting out everything. She could no longer hear the ticking of her heart, or Teddy's panicked whimpers. The terrible dark held dominion, and she saw *her*, obsidian eyes glittering with monstrous mirth.

In that moment, clarity chilled Tess's bones, stealing her breath. She'd escaped the nether world but, like a caged rat, the Sideways Lady had cornered Tess in her mind.

23

Round and Round

Dread lay dormant. Even when a prickle of something at the back of Tess's neck caused her heart to race and palms to sweat. Smiles disguised anguish and when Tess saw her reflection, she turned away, too afraid to see what her eyes might reveal.

She'd been home from Wales a few days, the cave of ghosts' experience consigned to an overblown imagination. Life resumed, or so Tess hoped, then she saw Teddy's drawings and buried dread rose like bile. All sleep-tousled hair, Teddy sat beneath his high-rise bed. He didn't look up. Hardly seemed to notice Tess as she walked into his room.

Somewhere in the neighbourhood, a lawnmower started up. Tess was glad of the noise, a distant hum breaking the terrible silence in Teddy's little bedroom.

"What are you drawing?" Tess's question was pointless. She recognised the grey of Sideways.

"A picture." Teddy rolled the pencil between his fingers. The lawnmower stuttered and died.

"What else did you draw, Teddy?"

Teddy opened his desk drawer full of paper sheets. Tess scanned the melancholy pictures. Pages and pages of the same bleak landscape. The images burned inside her mind.

In the scrawled sketch of tumultuous grey were two round circles. Darker grey—almost black—where the pencil had pressed hard.

"She's hiding there, somewhere. Watching. These are her eyes." Teddy continued his monotonous scribbling. Round and round, a sound that got inside Tess's head, reminding her of the moaning wind of Sideways, or the whooshing cloak of the Sideways Lady. Eerie. Like static. Filling all the gaps. Everywhere.

Tess groaned, her fingers digging into the faux leather of Teddy's chair. "Do you see her?"

"She talks to me in my dreams."

"What does she say?"

"She said that she's looking forward to seeing me again and she's 'specially looking forward to seeing you."

Round and Round the Sideways, like a teddy bear ...

"I won't let her have you, Teddy. I'll tell Mum and we'll work something out, okay?"

Round and round.

"Okay, Ted?"

Teddy slid Tess a glance. "Mum can't help. You can't either." He stopped scribbling and put his pencil down, unmoving, staring at nothing.

Blood drained from Tess's face. She released her grip on Teddy's chair, fingers cramping. *It's too late. I've already lost him.* Then, a surge of defiance swept over her. Teddy was ten. Not too late. She may have to do something drastic, or stupid, but she refused to give up. She couldn't bear to witness him suffering, Sideways inside his mind. Dreams slowly taking over his soul.

Mum would know what to do, despite what she said about Sideways being an urban legend. Something in her demeanour made Tess believe Mum had been lying. Perhaps she was trying to protect Tess, but Tess thought it more likely she was trying to pretend everything was okay. Mum was good at that.

The rules had changed, and Teddy needed help. *She needed help.* Suddenly, overwhelming despair weakened Tess as she saw her life spinning out of control at the mercy of the Sideways Lady. *Her pet.* Sludge bubbled inside. Rising. Choking. Tess just made it to the bathroom in time.

In bed, dreaming. Tess was Sideways, facing the clock shop, and there was the orange ball and green jerry can. The gate swung open, but she hesitated as incessant knocking disrupted the strange silence. She looked up. *Who was that banging on the window?* She stepped back, craning to see. Her own face stared down. Dream Tess shouted, pointing to the silver watch on her wrist. Wind howled, and the swirling, suffocating dirt of Sideways lifted from the earth.

Tess woke and groaned into her pillow. Through her bedroom window, grey twilight had snuffed out the day. She clutched the covers to her chin and closed her eyes knowing the dreams were real. That her subconscious mind stalked her. Cold understanding sneaked into her soul. She must return Sideways.

24

Memories and Lies

2 am. Tess stumbled from bed and slumped to the floor. She closed her eyes, listening to her breathing and the ticking of her heart. Her room was a sanctuary, the only place apart from Grandad's shop where she felt a sense of wellbeing. Dispelling anxiety. Relieving fear and pain.

A dusty memory hovered. Dad decorating, stringing up lights, and building a bookshelf with a crawl space beneath, where little Tess could snuggle up and read. 'It's hyggeligt,' he'd said in his soft Danish tone. '*Feels* cosy.'

Tess didn't know he would leave six months later. Even so, sitting on the floor, surrounded by familiar things, brought peace. The touch of fabric, a jumble of coloured buttons, the smell of old toys. Anything else was full of noise and chaos.

Tess gathered the objects about herself. Old diaries, teddies, trinkets, photos. Other memories stirred, but she felt no relief. Only a surge of distress. Looking for answers, she crept downstairs, hoping Mum would be up. It wasn't unusual for her to be awake in the early hours. Tess hated those nocturnal habits because Mum looked lost sitting alone in the glare of the TV. However, when Tess saw light oozing under the living room door, she felt like a little girl again, seeking comfort and solace in loving arms. The feeling soured, then disappeared.

Mum was knitting something red. Blood red like Samuel's ribbon. A plate scattered with crumbs and a half-eaten box of chocolates sat on the table by her side. The low drone of an old cop show flickered on TV.

Tired eyes fell upon Tess. A distracted smile. Busy fingers knitting. "What are you doing awake?"

"I might stay with Grandad for a bit."

The knitting stopped.

Tess perched on the edge of the sofa and studied the face she knew so well. Ghostly in the glare of the TV, and loose. *Like melting wax.* Tess shuddered. "Just a few days if you don't mind."

"So soon?"

"I enjoy it, and Grandad likes me there."

"Has this got anything to do with Ivor, because if it has, you'll never build a relationship with him if you go running off at the slightest hint of trouble?"

"I know and it's not that ..." Tess faltered, unsure how to say what was choking her.

"I know what you think of him," Jodie snapped. Knitting resumed, needles clacking in irritation.

"Do you?"

"You don't know what I see in him."

"Mum ..."

"I know he's not exactly ... I know he can be funny and a bit ..." *clack-clack-clack,* "but he loves me, and he's kind."

Tess sighed. "I know, Mum."

"After our first date, when I told him about you and Teddy, he was excited. He couldn't wait to meet you. I know he can never replace your real dad, but at least he won't run off!"

"This has nothing to do with Ivor, Mum."

"Oh. What then?"

"Why did you lie about living above the shop?"

The clacking stopped altogether. "What? I didn't."

What did Tess see in pale eyes? Like Grandad's, she realised. *Confusion? Fear?* "I was looking through some old photos, at ones when you were young. Remember how I used to make those awful collages?"

"Yes." A whisper.

"Well, there were pictures of you and Nan. I recognised the flat and courtyard. There was one of you sitting on the back step playing with dolls." Tess leaned forward as Jodie recoiled into the armchair's embrace. *Why did she seem so wary?*

"You lived there, didn't you?"

Jodie's frown deepened and her eyes glazed. "That's right, of course. Just a little while. In between houses."

Knitting needles trembled in veined hands. Something strange in Jodie's expression. *Fear?* Tess had to rethink. She'd never be allowed to return if there was a hint Sideways was real. Consigned as 'urban legend' for decades, there was a danger it might prove catastrophic for Mum's sanity. Time to back pedal.

"I'm fifteen and horology's my *thing*. Grandad's a good teacher, and it's important to think about my future."

"Yes, but something's been wrong since you got back. I don't like it there."

"How many times have I been to the shop over the years? Nothing's ever happened."

"Teddy isn't his usual self."

Tess pulled a face as though mocking her brother. "He believed it all! Grandad had no idea how frightened he was. A bit like Ivor and the ghost cave—" Tess paused for effect.

"But this business with the canal and all these questions."

An ad break came on TV. An overblown man with an irritating voice. Tess reached for the remote to mute him. "Imagination, Mum. You've always said reading all those Victorian horror books would give me nightmares."

"Not good for you," Jodie muttered.

Upstairs, Ivor coughed. Tess glanced at the ceiling. The bed creaked, then silence followed by snoring. A gurgling rumble. When she looked back, Jodie's face had a faraway expression. Tess noticed the dark gap in the bottom row of ageing teeth. From a distance, it looked like a black tooth.

Jodie's hands collapsed, as if her knitting needles had grown too heavy. "My friend Helen went to the dump. I'd forgotten about it until you mentioned it the other day."

Tess saw a picture of a curly-haired girl grinning beside young Jodie. Gaps in her smile. A black kitten between them.

With a sad shake of her head, Jodie sighed. "One day, I remember someone else answered her front door when I called. She'd moved. I never saw her again. Not long afterwards, we moved. The flat stayed empty for years until your nan and grandad moved back just after you were born."

"What happened to Helen, after she went Side—to the dump?"

"Nothing!" Jodie snapped, too impassioned. "Sideways *isn't* real. It's a fairy tale. A land of make-believe."

Jodie's fingers curled into white fists, and her pallid face changed. A childish pout replaced confusion. Sulking. Defiant in denial.

Tess reached for the TV remote and turned up the volume. The silence, punctuated by Ivor's snores, was too much to endure. For a moment she pretended to watch, but she didn't hear a word the man said. His voice seemed far away, and the room felt claustrophobic. A prison. Mum's indifference was agonising.

Tess had hoped for reassurance and a plan, but she was on her own. Her dream and Mary's belief that she was the one returned. Could Mum have stopped it when she was a child, or, like Teddy, been swallowed up? If Tess didn't try, what then? What happened when Grandad died, leaving the shop to the family? The Sideways Lady would always be their responsibility.

Ignoring the tingle of betrayal, Tess stroked Mum's chilly hands. "I can go, then?"

"How long for?"

Tess shrugged. "Not long. Be back before you know it."

Jodie traced the scar peeping above the collar of Tess's pyjama top, the familiar blanch of guilt scarring her face. Tess tried not to flinch, but it felt invasive. She needed to get away from those washed-out eyes.

"Night, Mum."

"Night."

"You know, I've never blamed you or Dad. It was an accident and because of it, I'm stronger. I'm *me*."

"Tess—"

"And another thing, I don't wear my boots to frustrate you. You know, don't you? I'm not trying to be someone else. I just like big boots." Tess reached for the door handle.

"Stay," Jodie whispered as canned laughter filtered from the TV.

"What—?" Tess turned back with a flutter of relief at her throat, but the laughing faces inside the TV mocked her. "Mum?"

Jodie didn't hear. She kept her gaze fixed on the screen, a half-smile on her pasty face. Tess must have imagined the plea. She fled upstairs, stifling a cry. Back inside a room that suddenly looked different, childish, but it wasn't the room that had changed. It was Tess. Tomorrow she would return to the clock shop. Leave childhood memories scattered across the bedroom floor and say goodbye.

25

Rav

Propelled towards MJ's Fish & Chips, Tess didn't know what she'd say when she got there. The morning sun warmed her on the path to the village. She hoped it might galvanise her, but no such luck.

After lingering across the road and being unable to see through the shop window, Tess crossed and loitered outside, hoping to glimpse Rav. The shop wasn't yet open, and they'd agreed to meet at four o'clock. Tess checked her watch. It was barely ten. Ivor had agreed to drive her back to Grandad's, but only if it tied in with his mid-morning squash. Frustrated and too shy to knock, Tess squirmed.

"You're early."

Rav's voice came from behind. Tess turned and met his broad smile. In his arms, he clutched shopping bags filled with potatoes.

"Hi," Tess said.

"You're not cancelling, are you?"

"Er …"

"Oh." The smile dropped, and he sighed.

"I don't want to—"

"Can I get rid of these?" Rav didn't wait for an answer but went to the door and pushed it open with his foot.

A middle-aged man appeared from inside. Another big smile, this time behind a moustache. He looked Tess up and down. "Ah, the girlfriend," he gushed.

"Uncle!" Rav blushed.

"Give me the bags and don't be standing around or your mama and auntie will come to eavesdrop. And don't be late for your shift!" The man winked at Tess.

"Must be cool working there. All those free chips."

Rav pulled a face, and it occurred to Tess he didn't have a choice. He was bullied at school because of the smell of fish and chips and oil. Some days, she smelled it too, but it never bothered her. There were so many other things about him. His eyes. That complexion. And he was fast and strong. With a start, Tess realised she was staring at his forearms. Rav pretended not to notice, but a grin graced his features.

Away from the quaint parade of shops, they turned a corner and headed to the park, where little kids played on swings and parents watched. Another Saturday morning playing out as it should be. Not for Tess, though. Maybe not for Rav, either.

"Sorry about my uncle."

Tess smiled. "Seems like a nice man."

"Yeah, a joker."

"You live there, don't you?"

Rav blushed again, and Tess wanted to kick herself. She had a feeling Rav was embarrassed about a lot more than just his clothes stinking of fish and chips.

"Yeah. Seven of us in two bedrooms." Rav stopped walking and turned to face Tess. "Is that why?"

"Why, what?"

"You're cancelling."

"What? No!"

"Oh. I thought—"

"You thought wrong, Rav. I don't care about any of that." Tess heard the passion in her voice. It was unexpected, and she fought tears. She strode on, suddenly anxious in his company.

They passed through big metal gates and sat on the roundabout. The metal was cold under Tess's fingers. Two gleeful children swung, tinkling laughter misplaced amid the gloom descending upon Tess.

"I can't make it this afternoon because I'm going back to Grandad's."

"Right, okay. Another time, then."

"I hope so," Tess mumbled.

Rav stood up. Instead of leaving, as Tess feared, he pushed the metal roundabout, broke into a trot, then jumped back on.

"I'm not letting you off until you tell me what's wrong."

Startled, Tess turned to him, trapped beneath his steady gaze. "I'm not ... I don't—"

"That day on the canal. You were frightened."

"Just embarrassed."

The roundabout slowed. Trees, children, a dog, slowly appeared, then disappeared as it turned.

Rav focused on his hands. "I was pushed into the canal at the beginning of term. It's cold and disgusting. An old lady with a little dog helped me climb out. That day I saw you was the first day I'd walked along the canal since."

"Who pushed you?"

With a frown, Rav studied Tess. He held her gaze, concern unmistakable in his luxurious eyes. His voice lowered. "The point is, I know what it's like to be embarrassed, but you were scared."

Tess felt a range of panicked emotions, but Rav sat there. Quiet. Patient. Caring. *Dare she tell him?* Defeated, she sighed. *Impossible.* The roundabout settled, and Tess gazed out across London's skyline. Haughty high-rise blocks of flats. Sleek lines of the Shard and the Gherkin. *Would it all be standing in another fifty years? Ten?* Even as she watched, smog clouded Tess's vision, and the buildings disappeared. Or perhaps it was the washed-out skirt of an invisible monster obliterating all.

"Tess?"

She hopped off the roundabout. "I came to tell you we can't meet later, but maybe, hopefully, some other time."

She stepped away, but Rav reached out and grabbed her hand. A spark ignited inside Tess's chest. Her body glowed, and a picture played inside her mind. Moments of time with Rav. Smiling. Laughing. Longing. A life she might live, but it wasn't hers. Not yet.

"I have to go."

Rav's voice was loaded with emotion. "Just tell me you're okay."

Tess smiled, checking a sob that almost strangled her. She tugged her hand free. "I'm okay, Rav. See you around."

It could have been a million miles walking back to the gate. Tess turned, ready to wave, but froze when she saw Rav. He stood by the roundabout, fists clenched, dark hair lifting from his forehead as a breeze blew across the playground. He took Tess's breath away. Tears fell and blurred her vision of this beautiful boy. As she turned, it occurred that this might be the last time she saw him.

The walk home was lonely. Life had changed irrevocably, and Tess was no longer who she'd always been. Or maybe the opposite. Maybe she *had* always been a warrior, but on the inside, hidden from view. Now she was the risen phoenix. She didn't want to be a warrior or a phoenix. Didn't want any of it. She longed to turn back time, to live in blissful ignorance and enjoy simple things and the company of a boy.

The memory of Rav's touch stilled Tess's heart, stopping the clock, but the further she walked, the more her heart resounded inside her chest. The steady beat of her life.

26

Wrong Time, Wrong Place

"The traffic will be busy," Ivor grumbled.

Tess ignored the dig and knocked on Teddy's bedroom door. He stood at the window, gazing into the grey garden. Drizzle obscured the view, merging sky and land into a bleak mass.

She looped an arm about Teddy's shoulders. "Why don't you sleep in my room while I'm gone, then you can look out the front window and be a nosy neighbour?" Tess poked him in the ribs.

"You mean it?"

Tess steered Teddy away from the window. "Only if you promise not to be alone, thinking of other things."

"You mean Sideways?"

"She can't get you here, Teddy."

Tess wanted to believe it, but over Teddy's shoulder, looking into the grey beyond, she felt an uneasy tingle.

Teddy flung himself at Tess, holding tight. He didn't notice her tears landing in his mop of hair.

Tess sniffed and blinked. "Ivor will be getting impatient."

"I have to give you something."

Untangling himself, Teddy climbed the ladder to his bed. He rummaged beneath his pillow and held out the war medal. Mum had threaded green ribbon through the original clasp, knotted it and made a necklace.

Teddy held it out. "You might need it."

Tess clutched the medal. "I'll keep it with me the whole time."

Downstairs, Mum seemed agitated. She offered her cheek for a kiss, then bundled Tess out the door. Once again, Tess ignored the niggle of betrayal and told herself it was better this way. She hurried to the idling car. Teddy would be standing at her bedroom window, but she didn't look to wave goodbye.

Tight-lipped, Ivor drummed podgy fingers on the steering wheel. He edged away from the kerb. "So, why are you going back to your grandad's? A little unusual, isn't it? Twice in the space of a few weeks?"

Tess leaned against the window, her reply a shrug and incoherent mumble. She closed her eyes and thought of Rav. Ivor's scathing tone broke through her reverie.

"I know you dislike me." Stony-faced, Ivor stared ahead, bulging eyes clear, even in profile.

Tess frowned. "Don't be silly, Ivor."

Traffic lights turned red. Ivor eased on the brakes, hitched on the handbrake, and turned to Tess. "That day in the cave ..."

"Can we forget that?"

"I need to understand the crux of the matter. If you can explain, then I'll happily forget it."

Tess glared. *You were an idiot.* "Doesn't matter now."

Ivor's stubby thumbs danced against the steering wheel. "Had you done what I said and persuaded Teddy to jump down, we could have avoided that situation. As it was, you encouraged his irrational behaviour, and he no longer trusts me."

"Lights are green," Tess muttered, anger heating her cheeks.

The car crawled before stopping again. Tess considered opening the door and leaping free, but the fallout would be exhausting.

"What do you have to say, Tess?"

Tess chewed on the inside of her cheek. Ivor was like a sanctimonious science teacher at school.

"Well?" Ivor waited. Fishlike. Blinking.

Unable to mask her fury, Tess glowered. "I don't think we should talk about this without Mum. If you want to discuss it as a family, get to the *crux* of the matter, then we can decide if looking out for my ten-year-old brother scared silly by your cave of ghosts was irresponsible."

Ivor puffed out his chest, lips pursed in irritation. He didn't say another word as the car stop-started all the way to the clock shop. Tess clambered out.

"Am I picking you up on Monday?"

"I'll catch the bus."

"I don't mind."

Tess smiled through gritted teeth. "Great, thanks."

Glad to be away from the car's confines and awkward conversation, Tess ambled to Grandad's shop and paused outside. Everything was as it should be. Peeling black paint on the door. Georgian windows patterned in cobwebs. The regal sign with its golden fob watch image. The street itself, hiding from London, its many memories and age-old secrets stitched together with cobbled stones. All familiar, yet something sinister lay beyond.

Tess pushed open the door, smiling at the jingle, and for a moment, remembered everything she loved about being here. The smell. Gloom. The comforting ticking. But they faded to nothing and all she could see was *her* filling Grandad's chair. Even the squishy blue armchair, forever tainted by Mary and her filthy rags.

Grandad emerged from the kitchen wiping his hands on a cloth, but there was no sparkle in the blue eyes. He stood beside his desk. "You're late."

"Always am." Tess pecked his ruddy cheek and plucked the dull star from her pocket. It dangled from the ribbon, spiralling.

"Teddy took this home. I didn't know."

"I told him he could look after it for a while." Grandad poked the medal, making it swing.

"I'll keep it for now." Tess tucked the battered medal away. She liked its heaviness. Liked what it represented. Perhaps she could absorb courage from it.

"Your mum told me you wanted to spend more time here. I think *you* need to tell me why you're really here, don't you?"

Tess looked around the shop. At the shadows hiding in dark corners. *Where was her courage?* "Can we go upstairs?"

Without a murmur of hesitation, Grandad crossed to the front door, turned the latch, and changed the shop sign to closed.

Tess trudged upstairs and headed to the bright yellow kitchen. She sat down and waited, listening to creaking stairs as Grandad climbed. Or was it old bones? Tess couldn't imagine him growing old and dying, but he was already old.

"Tea?"

"Sure."

"How was Wales?"

Tess saw the glint in his eyes. "I'm not sure I like Ivor much."

"No. Understandable."

Tess experienced a rush of affection. Grandad filled the hole in her life, and she wasn't sure he knew. Not that he didn't challenge her sometimes, but he treated her as an equal and spoke as he felt.

"Perhaps he doesn't like you much either." The old man chuckled and plopped down in a seat opposite.

"I'm not even sure Mum likes him. He's safe, she says."

"Your mum was vulnerable after your dad left. Ivor *is* safe."

Tess had a flashback to the cave. "He's no pushover, that's for sure. Unpredictable too. Sulky."

"Like a teenager?"

Tess laughed. "I prefer it here to home, you know."

She looked around the little kitchen. At the obsolete cookware faded in layers of dust displayed along the cupboard tops. At last year's calendar hanging from a nail on the wall, and the many gouges in the old kitchen table. Tess's thoughts turned to the shop downstairs. Once her sanctuary. "At least I did."

Grandad flinched, but Tess didn't want to hide anything. Not that she could convey much. All she knew was a feeling of being upside down. Inside out. Since the day she'd seen Teddy's drawings, or perhaps it was the canal, Sideways was everywhere. If only she could believe Mum was right and Sideways was a fairy story of old. Malevolent, disturbing, but merely a tale to terrify children.

"What was the rhyme, Grandad?" Tess hated herself for taking away well-deserved peace, but he was all she had.

The old man's whisper was barely audible over the sound of the kitchen clock. A steadfast, lopsided old thing hanging on the wall. "Sideways creeps and crawls and waits. Run away from its hellish gates."

Tess licked dry lips, the chilling words filling her mind. "That's what it's like. Crawling, waiting, and its hellish gates are right here. Outside."

"Then why did you come back?"

Tess went to the window, her breath steaming the glass. "I used to see the dump out there, nothing more, but things have changed. *Sideways* has changed."

Tess reeled away to face Grandad. He'd slumped, the flesh of his jowls hanging loose. A sign he was concentrating, or exhausted, his flesh blotched red and purple. More like blueberry pie than cold, malleable dough. A face she loved.

"All these years this shop has stood quietly on this spot, the same Victorian streets outside. It's as though the past hundred years haven't happened. I think that's why I love it so much. A little world that exists outside the real one or nestled in a corner, hidden away."

Despite pain-filled eyes, Grandad smiled. He felt it too. "It gets noisy in the real world."

"When the Knocker-Upper woke *her* up, she started in motion. This *energy* that has gathered momentum, eating up time as though it doesn't exist. All to get to this point, and I think …" Tess paused.

"What do you think?"

Tess couldn't deny instinct, more powerful than fear. "I feel like I'm in the *middle* of the story. That time has settled on me."

Tess ignored the horror mirrored in the blue sky of Grandad's eyes and took a sip of tea. Something stirred within her. *Acceptance?* Easier in daylight, perhaps, but she'd try to hold on to the feeling. As Grandad cleared his throat to protest, Tess stopped him.

"I saw Dad a few days ago, but it wasn't him. *She* tricked me into seeing something that wasn't there. If I hadn't realised, I'd think I might've been lost."

"But you did realise and you're safe now."

Tess reached for leathered hands. "Teddy sees her all the time. In his dreams. I wish I could ignore it all, but I'm afraid things won't ever be the same for us."

"In time, they will. You must be patient."

Tess saw Ivor's face float before her. Pasty and bloated in the cave's gloom. "Wait for *what*? She changes what I see."

"But, my dear, what on earth do you think you can do?"

Tess laughed. A pitiful, disconsolate sound. "Don't know. I really have no clue."

"Run *away* from its hellish gates, Tess. That's what the rhyme says, remember?"

Tess saw desperation in Grandad's eyes. In the way he reached out to her. She allowed him to clasp her hands, urging her to run away, but the Tess in her dream had made it clear. The barren world outside drew her attention again. Unchanging, endless landscape, and in the distance, the crumbling asylum.

Afraid, Tess whispered. "*There's nowhere to run to. All the clocks say the same thing and here I am. Wrong time. Wrong place.*"

27

Tess of the Clock Shop

It wasn't long before the uncertainty of having no clue took its toll on Tess. She knew something had to happen but couldn't think what. Plunging into the grey of Sideways without a plan was madness. That's all she was sure of. Without magic to save the day, Tess knew she was out of her depth, knee-deep in despair.

Loving and attentive as he was, Grandad was the opposite of helpful. He tiptoed around, trying to draw Tess into conversations about anything other than Sideways, but it was hopeless. She couldn't eat. Couldn't read. Couldn't function at all. She felt sluggish, half alive, and the clocks ticked on until Tess imagined them marching her towards her doom.

When sleep came, it brought bulging shadows in her mind. When awake, they bulged in the dark corners of her bedroom. She tossed and turned, but the darkness wanted to play games. Exhausted, Tess waited for dawn, watching ghoulish faces appear amid the flowers of thin yellow curtains.

Her nerves were in tatters when she heard a tap against the window. Tugging the blankets over her head, she resisted the childish desire to scream for Grandad. Perhaps she'd imagined it. If she ignored it, the sound would go away. Under the covers, she heard another muffled tap.

Tess emerged, feeling a wave of shame. *What if there was a logical explanation?* She thought of the war medal under her pillow and eased a corner of the curtain aside. Clad in pyjamas, in the twilight of Sideways, a small figure hurled stones at the glass. Teddy was out there. He waved, but there was something strange in his countenance. Something un-Teddy like.

Tess reached for her dressing gown and hurtled downstairs with no other thought than Teddy was Sideways again. The kitchen was dark. She flicked the switch, and a yellow glow ambushed the gloom. The stiff bolt moved reluctantly in the locked door, metal grinding metal. Tess flew across the courtyard and yanked open the gate. Sideways gusted, lapping at her feet, its acrid smell burning.

"Teddy!" Tess cried, but she was alone.

There was something dreamlike about the night. Tess glanced up at the window. A patch of light illuminating the house, the gap in the curtain watchful. Perhaps she was still up there, peering down at herself. A troubling thought.

Tess turned away. "Teddy, are you here?" Tess's voice echoed. *Definitely a dream.*

If she was dreaming, there was nothing to fear. She reached out, wanting to claw the shadowy night towards her and rip it apart, but it whipped about her face, cruel and cold. The stink stole her breath.

Tess stumbled. In the distance, she saw Grandad's back gate and the narrow house beyond, gobbled up by Sideways, just as the Sideways Lady gobbled up the pieces of clock and watch. Swallowing time. This was no dream. The Sideways Lady had tricked her and was here, watching. Tess knew she must move. Retreat to safety.

Impossible at first, but then Tess imagined being lost forever, one day turning to dust. Her feet came to life. She darted back through the courtyard, accidentally kicking the orange ball, which bounced off the green jerry can. Inside, she fumbled to lock the door, then leaned against it, finding her breath. She told herself she was safe, while not believing she was.

Seeking comfort, Tess staggered into the shop, but a terrible smell obliterated the ticking. A movement in the shadows. Weak and afraid, she clutched the doorframe. *She had a visitor.* For a moment, Tess thought about fleeing, but where would she run? She'd returned to the clock shop knowing she may have to face the creature of Sideways. Just not so soon.

There *she* sat, a nightmare in the gloom. The flesh of her bloated face rippled as she turned to Tess and smiled. A cockroach dropped from her mouth, its armour glowing amber as it scurried across the desk in a frantic bid for freedom. Fascinated, the fiend stared, then slammed her hand down, crunching the bug's bone and shell. With awkward fingers, she scooped the crushed, oozing roach into her horrifying mouth.

Tess looked at the narrow staircase, thinking she may find safety where Grandad lay sleeping, where there was a kitchen with knives. With her back to the wall, she edged towards the stairs. The Sideways Lady sniggered like a gurgling drain. Tess muttered a prayer, but even while praying, she knew she stood alone.

Brutish hands plucked, then dropped a thin chime from the desk. It clattered to the table with a doleful hum. "Hmm. Pleasing. I like it here. Shall I stay?"

"What do you want?"

Eyes flashing with an unnatural glimmer studied Tess. "I think you know."

An icy shiver shot down Tess's spine. "Don't hurt me," she pleaded.

"Hurt you? Why ever would I hurt you? I choose you for my own, but you seem disinclined to stay with me."

The Sideways Lady appraised Tess, an ugly half-smile upon her fleshy face. She stood, gathering her rotten aura, edging across the floor in jerky movements.

Please let me be dreaming. The stench was too much, and the creature lurched closer. "You know, don't you, Tess of the Clock Shop, that it's different for you?"

Trapped against the wall, Tess recalled the man, not her dad. Ivor's ghoulish mask in the cave. Sideways, but not. She nodded, trembling still.

"Tell me, Tess," the creature mumbled into her ear.

"You make me see things."

"I can make everyone see things, but you aren't fooled like some, though I nearly had you, didn't I? At the canal. The old hag's the same, but you. You fascinate me. A child, but with a streak of something making you shine." She edged closer, malleable face rippling with unseen horrors, hungry eyes roving over Tess. "*I like shiny things.*"

Despite the wall behind her, Tess recoiled, defeated. "Please …"

"I could take you now, if I chose, but I want you to come to me."

The Sideways Lady toyed, smiling, showing cherrystone teeth and grey gums. She tilted her head and, with a child's fascination, slowly extended a hand towards Tess's neck, mirroring the shape of the faded scar. A shape like clawing fingers.

"I am inside your head, and the boy's, but I'll swap you for him. Come to me and I will release him from Sideways. Sever the cord joining them." She drew her grey tongue over her bottom lip, wetting her chin.

I'll swap you for him. Tess groaned, afraid, and with an urgent desire not to die. A touch from a fat finger sent a jolt of revulsion through her body. The creature was tracing her scar.

"Please," Tess begged, pain splintering somewhere inside.

The monstrous form blurred, but Tess could still see a fragment of gleeful mouth as she reached inside of Tess, beyond the scar of her skin, through flesh and bone.

"I don't want to hurt you, Tess. I want to be your friend. We're alike, you and I. Lonely and different. Will you come?"

"I'll come."

Another smile, mad and cruel. With a contented sigh and a slight nod, the Sideways Lady shrivelled upon herself and became a vapour of stink. Then she was gone.

Eventually, Tess's tremors lessened, replaced by a feeling of shame. In time, she noticed the quiet ticking of every clock. She slid down the wall, hugging her knees close. Not even sleep would absolve her of the hellish nightmare that awaited.

28

Redemption, After All?

Tess woke late, feeling drained. The narrow bed with its faulty springs provided refuge. Buried under the covers, thinking of nothing much, sleep called her back. She ignored the temptation.

In the mirror, the Sideways Lady stared back, amusement reflected in obsidian eyes. Tess washed, scrubbing at her cheeks, but a glossy sheen plastered her flesh white. She cringed, remembering the tracing of her scar, the pain nearly bringing her to her knees. She'd returned to the clock shop hoping to fix her broken brother, and *she* had made an offer. *I'll swap you for him.* For Tess, there'd be no redemption. She watched Grandad pottering around the kitchen, his body protesting as it did every morning. Tess felt detached from him. *Why couldn't he see what happened? Why wasn't he looking?* Resigned, Tess sighed. She wouldn't tell him. That would destroy him. Like termites, her words would burrow inside until there was nothing left.

"I've run out of eggs," he chirped.

"It doesn't matter, Grandad."

He opened the fridge and peered inside. "I'm not having my granddaughter go without her eggs. I don't have milk either. Not enough for all the tea you drink, anyway," he chuckled.

"Shall I go and buy some?" Wearily, Tess got to her feet. She didn't know anyone who drank as much tea as Grandad.

"I have a better idea. I'll treat you to breakfast."

The idea of breakfast seemed obscene.

"I'm quite happy with toast."

"Ah, well, it appears I have no bread, either."

"I'll get my boots."

They walked in silence. The shining sun seemed obscene too.

"The traveller rarely traverses this part of London, you know."

Tess was only half-listening.

Grandad looked about, glazed eyes bluer than usual in the sunshine. "It's funny. A city so overrun with traffic and tourists can have areas many never see. I've always loved Her. The old streets. The buildings. You know Dickens Row, of course, in the other direction. The original Old Curiosity Shop stood there. So history has it."

Tess did know. Nan had taken her to the shop once. It was called Old and Curious now, and the elderly owner who emerged from the shadows of the ancient shop was himself, old and curious.

"There's something about the greyness of London that inspires my soul. I know people find it dirty and overrun, but there's history beneath our feet, Tess."

Tess glanced at Grandad. Was he trying to tell her something?

He smiled uneasily. "I know these streets like the back of my hand and would never take a wrong turn, of course."

"You mean go Sideways?"

A frown. "You know, Tess, I've lived through some exciting times, but time can be cruel. People die, get forgotten, but Sideways ..."

The old man faltered, and Tess saw how frail and ancient he appeared. A Dickens character. Smart attire, but dusty and dishevelled. Pinched in the face and red in the nose. He took out a handkerchief, blew, then walked on, the sound of his shoes ringing out upon the hard stone.

"Sideways is a shadow over London and there are those that say it's changing the fabric of our streets. That one day, this great city will change beyond recognition."

Something caught Tess's eye. She paused, peering into a narrow alleyway that was so dark it faded to nothing. An aroma of rotting rubbish spewed from the gloom. A bin toppled. Rats probably. Tess was afraid of rats. They were everywhere in London, never more than five feet away. Giant vermin. Monstrous. A shadow crept from the depths and Tess heard a whisper carried towards her. She stepped towards the sound, then stumbled as the cornered creature hissed, flashing deadly splinters of teeth and red eyes.

"Tess?" She felt Grandad's hand upon her arm. "Are you okay?"

The alleyway was empty. The dark, benign.

"Thought I saw a rat." Tess muttered, suddenly cold.

Plunging his hands into deep coat pockets, Grandad hunched against the morning chill. They strolled on, his footsteps echoing in the narrow street. He halted, a smile straining through the wrinkles. "We're here."

Tess glanced at the café's dreary façade. Saw a woman behind the counter, peering out, expectant. *More than just breakfast?* Tess's memory of the night before faded in the glow of daylight. She'd offered herself up for Teddy's soul, but perhaps there was an alternative. If she returned Sideways to do the bidding of a soulless entity wandering the bleak paths of hell, what future would she have? If she had a chance to save her own soul, she'd take it. *Redemption, after all?*

29

Dot's Café

Outside Dot's Café, a closed red door faced Charlie Smith and Tess. Glancing through a picture window, Tess spied one lady sitting alone, nursing an empty mug. Her frothy hair had the colour of candyfloss. She looked up, small eyes narrowed. Tess had the unnerving sensation the woman was waiting for her. Behind the counter stood another woman. Red hair, red lips, tea towel slung over one shoulder.

"Me and your nan came here all the time. Dot makes the best bacon sandwiches, and you can drink as much tea as you like. Come on."

Tess followed him to the counter.

"Charlie Smith! What a sight for sore eyes."

He allowed the woman to embrace him. Dot, Tess presumed. The woman smiled, flashing teeth resembling uncooked chips.

Charlie squirmed, discomfort clear from the russet flush in his cheeks. "This is my granddaughter, Tess."

"Of course she is." The woman's eyes belied her fixed smile.

Tess glanced over her shoulder at candyfloss hair watching her. The woman put an empty mug to pink lips. *I think they're both waiting for me.*

"What can I get you?" Dot asked.

Tess scanned a sticky menu. *All day breakfast at your friendly NEIGHbourhood café.* "Egg on toast, please."

She parked herself at one of the cracked red tables. Sad salt and pepper pots slouched between weary bottles of tomato ketchup and brown sauce.

"Nice place," Tess sneered, taking in the tired décor and empty chairs. She imagined the place once bustled with life. Tourists passing through, enjoying a cuppa before a day's sightseeing. Nan and Grandad sitting by the window, watching the world go by. Not that much happened on the streets outside. Perhaps all the action had been inside.

Grandad released a heavy sigh. "Your nan would be cross with me for not coming back here. We always enjoyed people-watching."

Dot brought two mugs of steaming tea. She touched Tess's face with calloused fingers. "She looks like her nan." Her voice held an unmistakable sound of sorrow. The two women must have been good friends.

"We all look the same. Nan, Mum, and me."

Dot frowned. "Yes, of course. Jodie's girl."

For a moment, Dot seemed lost, fixated on something only she could see, then she flashed ugly teeth and scurried back to the kitchen.

"She's a bit strange, Grandad."

"Dot's always been odd. She was quite close to your nan. I think she's one of those spiritual people, you know?" He whispered as if *spiritual* were a rude word and gestured to the other woman who sat peering into the depths of her bag. "She's another one. Mad as hatters, I always thought, but your nan was good at picking friends she could rely on."

As if she'd heard, the frothy-haired lady looked over, waggling bejewelled fingers. Rings on every digit except stubby thumbs.

"Why did you come back, Tess? I know you're planning something."

Tess sipped her tea, then pulled a face. "No plan, Grandad."

"You asked me before, had I always wanted to be a horologist. It was my passion. I learned how to put a watch back together before I was seven years old. It's all I ever wanted to be."

Tess leaned forward, lowering her voice. "I heard Sideways doesn't affect you if you know inside who you are. That you can smell it and know what it is."

Grandad's eyes flashed, then he startled Tess by thumping his fist down. Disturbed by the weight, salt scattered across the table. "Exactly! You're the same. You can smell the danger."

Tess dashed the sparkling salt crystals to the floor. "Things have changed. It's spreading. And *she's* getting stronger."

No need to tell Grandad that *her* smell could make you lose yourself. Or that she'd selected Tess as a special friend. A pet. She cast the thoughts aside, her new resolve to show no weakness.

The old man flopped back in his chair. "I went looking for her once."

Suddenly uncomfortable under Grandad's scrutiny, Tess shifted in her seat. Here was a different man. Eyes blazing and a memory twisting his mouth into a gruesome line. Creaking bones were sharp angles. No smile in sight. No warmth. Tess waited, trapped.

"I was older than you are and arrogant. Most people said she was nothing more than an urban myth. Even so, people knew to stay away. It was always so bleak. A few steps Sideways was like being lost at sea."

Tess took a sip of tea, glad to look away, but Grandad kept on, his gravelled voice a low drone.

"I *knew* it was more than legend, but I felt invincible and because of me, because of my arrogance, I nearly lost my best friend."

"I don't understand why you're telling me this, Grandad."

As though the memory grew too big, the pain too great, Grandad's face rippled in anguish. He drew a trembling hand across his mouth to suppress a sob. "I'm telling you because I was like you, but it's tortured me from that day to this."

"You have Sideways inside you?" Tess trembled, the thought too horrible to conceive, but Grandad shook his head.

"No. Sideways never got me. But it got my friend, Ben Butler. He played cricket before ..."

For a moment, Charlie Smith disappeared inside his mind. What could he see? The café was still and silent, as though time had halted. Tess turned to look at the candyfloss lady and met her pitying stare. In the kitchen, something heavy fell, startling the old man back to life.

"We had a metal bin in the back yard and before we left, I'd dragged it outside our gate to light a fire in it. Pretty normal thing to do in those days, but it meant we could get home. So long as we could see the fire, we'd find our way. We'd joked about it beforehand, but it saved our lives."

Charlie's intense gaze settled on Tess. He was afraid for her. Understandable. Elsewhere, far away from the dingy café, the city was alive. Londoners had traversed the same cobbled streets for centuries. Soulful. Life-giving. Streets with a heartbeat that Tess felt from an early age. Held aloft by Grandad. Counting bridges. Counting people. *And now?* She felt unsafe and unsure of herself. Rats hid in corners and Death waited, scythe raised. Life, once determined and secure, had morphed into something intangible. A future glimpsed through a dirty window.

"What happened to your friend afterwards, Grandad?"

"The point is Teddy's young. He'll be fine away from here and with you looking out for him."

Tess pictured Teddy's frenzied scribbles. "I want to believe that."

Dot emerged from the kitchen with breakfast. Her footsteps stuck to the tacky floor.

"Thanks," Tess murmured.

"You're welcome." Dot glanced at Charlie, unspoken words passing between them.

Tess picked up a knife and fork. The food smell tickled her nostrils, making her hungrier than she'd been in a while. She didn't want to talk about Sideways anymore. Would have liked to pretend she and Grandad were enjoying breakfast together. With staring eyes upon her, Tess shovelled egg into her mouth.

She glared at candyfloss, who had the decency to look away. "I feel like an exhibit."

Grandad creaked closer. "The scourge of Sideways has been part of London life for over a century. But we survive, like we survived the war. Most of us. As for *her* ..." he hesitated, stricken.

"Grandad?"

"Make no mistake, Tess. She's a monster. A ruthless monster, and it isn't right that it should fall upon your shoulders, but that's why you came back, isn't it? Because of a misguided sense of duty?"

Instantly, the egg on Tess's plate didn't appeal.

The old man reached out, clasping her hands. "Tolstoy said that the two most powerful warriors are patience and time. True words. *Please*, go home and consider with care. Take your time. *Be patient.*"

Green eyes met blue. "What if I'm the only one who can stop this? You said yourself London will change. That the entire world will be in danger."

"But it's not your responsibility, Tess! And consider this. What if, in thinking you can help, you're putting yourself and Teddy in more danger?" Haggard in body, strong of mind but grown weary, Charlie Smith collapsed back. Creaking chair. Creaking bones. He picked up his knife and fork with delicate precision. "Finish your food. There's someone I'd like you to meet."

Breakfast, not breakfast.

Tess ploughed through her food and gulped a second cup of tea. She heard laughter outside. People playing out their lives. London wasn't far away at all, and the sun was shining. A normal day. Normal things happening. Grandad wanted her to meet someone and willingly, she would. She didn't want to go Sideways again and that was the reality.

Here was an enticing alternative. The idea sparkled inside Tess's mind. A glimmer of hope shining within the shadows of her soul.

30

Book of Names

With a steely gaze fixed on Tess, Grandad drained his tea, then got to his feet. "I'll leave you to it and don't need to tell you to come straight home. No detours along the way, eh?"

"Wait. You're leaving?"

"Trust them," he entreated, called thanks to Dot, and left.

Tess squirmed in her seat but resisted the urge to dash after him. This unchartered path required an open mind. The two women might give her nothing. Or everything. She had to look past dour expressions and eccentric appearance.

Suddenly formidable, Dot wasted no time. She marched to the door, flicked the sign to closed, then put her hands on her hips. "Tess, meet Helga."

Helga gathered an oversized handbag to her breast and scurried over. Despite the façade of fluffy pink hair and matching slippers, she wore a fierce expression, rigid lines deeply entrenched. She was small. Barely five-foot, Tess guessed. In normal circumstances, Tess would have found her amusing, but these weren't normal circumstances.

Glowering, Helga dropped into the seat opposite. Tess didn't crack a smile.

"She's like her grandmother, isn't she?" Helga said to Dot, the German accent unmistakable. She clicked her tongue as if Tess didn't deserve such an accolade. "So, we're here to help you understand what you don't understand. Do you understand?"

"I'm not sure."

Dot eased into the chair next to Tess. "Helga, please don't go on too much."

Helga fixed Tess with her fierce gaze. "As you know, Sideways has become a problem, and, thanks to you, the Sideways Lady, more of a problem."

"Pardon?"

"*Baba Jaga*. You led her to your grandfather's shop and now she has a taste for things outside of Sideways."

"Helga," Dot warned.

Helga's small grey eyes glowed with unexpected warmth. "She can never fully pass to this side, however."

Dot leaned in. "She's bound by Sideways."

Tess could still feel the cold of the canal, the slime beneath her fingertips, and didn't believe them.

Dot saw Tess's fear. "She's a monster, Tess. You're a child. Not a worthy adversary."

"What do I do?"

Helga snorted. "What do you do? Nothing, of course!"

"Go home. Pick up the pieces and live your life." The red tea towel hung like a damp scarf over Dot's shoulder.

"But what about my brother? He changed when he went Sideways."

Helga rummaged in her bag, produced a thick notebook, and licked her finger. With pink fingernails and a flourish, she opened the book in the middle, then cleared her throat. Small eyes darted about, first at Tess, then at Dot, then back to the book. "Sally Plum. Anne Hempstead. Ivan Smith. Douglas Smith."

"Helga—"

"Irene Finch. Jason Car—"

"Helga!"

Helga snapped the book closed and cast a withering glance at Dot. "I'm trying to make a point."

"Perhaps if you showed Tess your book of names, she'd get the idea."

Bristling, Helga slid the notebook across the table to Tess. "The names you see are people who went Sideways over the years and lived to a good age."

Tess flicked through the book. Countless names. Pages of them. "They all lived normal lives?"

Helga glanced at Dot. "Yes. More or less."

What did that look mean? Tess narrowed her eyes. Dot wouldn't even look at her.

"What do you mean? More or less."

Helga snatched the book away. "Even people who don't go Sideways don't always make the most of their lives."

Impossible to argue logic.

"Dot and I believe the best thing you can do is leave London. Underneath an open sky, it will be easier to ignore."

Hope kindled and warmed Tess as she closed her eyes. If they left London, they could live in Wales. Ivor would love that, and Mum wouldn't need much convincing. Teddy would be okay. No more drawings.

She'd been a fool to listen to Mary. These two old ladies understood she had no chance against the creature without a soul. Behind closed lids, Tess felt free. She clung to the feeling. Sideways wasn't her problem and, with her indomitable stink, Baba Jaga, as Helga called her, would fade into nothing. Until then, merely a lingering smell. A half-remembered nightmare. Tess could live with that. Not half a life, but full.

31

The Old Quarter

Tess wrestled with the moment of peace. What might happen when life settled still? When she was alone with only the ticking of her heart?

Helga stared. What could Tess see? Not concern, or pity, but knowledge and truth. She'd seen the same intensity in Mary's gaze. Looking into those eyes revealed more than words could.

Tess focused on the world outside. The sun gave everything a mellow glow, but she recalled the bite of cold against her flesh. The warm glare was a lie. The rat she'd seen—not imagined—and its whispered warning. *Sideways creeps and crawls and waits.* If they moved to Wales, she could pretend to live a normal life, but not forever. Not for long.

"You have a question?" Dot lifted badly-drawn eyebrows.

"What about Ben Butler?"

"Why do you ask about him?" Helga snapped.

"He was Grandad's friend. His name should be in your little book."

"Well, Helga? Tess wants to know about Ben Butler."

Dot's face had a peculiar look. Curious, bemused. She watched Tess as Helga flicked through the pages, the blur of names turning red towards the end of the book.

Helga moved her finger down the list. She mumbled, flicked back a page, then another, before stabbing with a pink, pointed nail. "Ben Butler. Dead."

"How old was he?" Tess muttered.

Helga wriggled in her seat. "I don't have that information."

"How old, Dot?"

Dot shrugged, flashing a rueful smile. "Not sure. He died before his parents. Forty, maybe?"

"What does it matter? Everybody dies."

"Everybody dies," Tess repeated.

A storm raged inside Tess's head. Helpless, the two old women watched on. Heavy silence fell. No movement, no words, then a faraway sound. A man's voice calling out. Tess recognised the jarring tone of a street seller and wondered what he was selling. She puffed out a sigh, breaking the spell.

Dot lay her hand upon the book, easing it to herself. She turned to the first page and trapped Tess in her gaze. "There are some who never leave Sideways. Who fall asleep and stay there forever."

Tess swallowed the lump and fought against an anguished sob. *Did they know about Alice?*

"Martin Turner. He was the first," Dot said, pointing to the looped letters of his name in old-fashioned handwriting.

Helga spluttered. "What are you doing, Dot?"

"What am I doing? Improvising."

"We agreed to help!"

Dot studied Tess, and a warm smile grew on her face. "Charlie didn't tell us how much like Irene their granddaughter was. She's too smart to believe us, telling her what she *wants* to hear. She needs to know the truth."

"I think I know the truth."

"We can help you," Dot said.

Tess scraped back her chair. In her desire to get away, she almost stumbled. Anger was building. A storm raging still. She paced to the door but couldn't leave yet. Too many unanswered questions. She turned back. "This is all mad. I don't even know you. Who are you?"

"The Guardians of Sideways."

Dot rolled her eyes. "Helga's being dramatic, love, but we *are* part of the triangle that keeps Sideways sideways. The clock shop, this café, and Helga's pub, The Old Gin Palace, make up this forgotten part of London. The Old Quarter, back in the day. Nothing much has changed in over a century. All those narrow streets near Blackbird Lane and Dickens Row. Same cobbles, same buildings. Secrets buried underfoot, memories ingrained in the damp and dark. They are ghost walks now. Tourists come wanting to see a ghost, not realising the spirits are there all the time. Watching."

Dot reclined in the old wooden chair and looked around. Her eyes settled on a series of old photo frames on the wall. "This place used to be a blacksmiths. Still has an old stable out the back. Sometimes, I hear the clang of metal."

Tess eased back into the chair to listen to Dot. Her words wielded power over the chaos in Tess's mind.

"History isn't something that happens and disappears behind us. Moments grow roots and run deep, like this place. I can smell the iron burning, a smell like earth and fire." Dot's eyes wandered. She was there, feeling the flames' heat, eyes fixed on Helga.

"On warm nights, with my window open, I hear the Great Fire crackle. It started in Pudding Lane. Near my pub. Sometimes, the screaming wakes me," Helga said.

Tess shivered. "When the asylum burnt down, I imagined all that pain and suffering lifting free, like ash."

"The more terrible the moment, the deeper roots run," Dot said.

Tess glanced over her shoulder. Outside, the sun was high in the sky. "Does that mean Sideways lies beneath London?"

"That's our best guess. Here and there it's glimpsed from the corner of your eye, but London is weak, and its history's being stripped from the streets. That's why we three are more vital than ever before."

Tess frowned at Dot. "What do you mean?"

Helga replied. "This café is opposite my pub. As the crow flies. Charlie's shop is the apex of the triangle. For whatever reason, the three buildings have always been the barrier."

"The clock shop's on Barricade Street," Tess mumbled.

"No coincidence," Helga said.

"But now, it appears there are new rules. Still, we knew one day someone would come along to stop it."

Tess met Dot's gaze as a tremor passed through her. "And that someone is me?"

"No," Helga barked.

Dot glared at Helga. "I know Charlie wanted us to tell her she didn't need to go. That Teddy would be okay if they left London, but honestly, Helga, what good does that do? I think it's time she was sent back to sleep, don't you?"

"Dot!" Horrified, Helga's stubby fingers clutched her enormous bag.

"We're getting old, Helga. Charlie too, and *she's* crossed the line. Mary made it perfectly clear—"

"Wait a minute. You know Mary?" Tess said.

Dot wrinkled her nose. "Yes, we know Mary. She's been advising us for many years. And our mothers and grandmothers. She comes, bringing her stink, tells us what's what then leaves again."

"And what has she told you about me?"

Dot leaned across the table and clutched Tess's hand. "She said you were scared, love. Pretending to yourself that you didn't feel it inside, that the Sideways Lady thinks you belong together. She thinks you're the same."

Tess snatched her hand away. "But that's ridiculous. How can I be like her? I'm *nothing* like her."

"No, you're not, but she thinks you are, and that's why she may never leave you alone, regardless of where you go," Helga said.

The uneasy peace that had settled dispersed, fear threatening to drag Tess into its murky depths. She rose from her chair again. "But you said out of London would be safe. You read out those names of people who lived normal lives."

Dot stood and held Tess's shoulders. "None of them had the Sideways Lady around for a visit, Tess."

"Why does she think we're the same?" Tess cried.

As though a great weight was upon her, Dot released Tess and fell back into her chair. But Tess saw the direction of Dot's gaze. She looked between the women, her mind swimming with injustice.

"My *scar*?"

Helga mumbled in reply. "We don't know."

"She thinks we've got stuff to talk about because of my scar." Tess laughed, choking back a sob.

"Our best guess," Dot said.

The scar. An identity tag. It had taken Tess a long time to realise it didn't define her but gave her something to build upon. From the embers, she'd grown strong and courageous. Assured of the person she could become. At the same time, she felt it had driven her parents apart. A blessing and a curse.

Mesmerised by the shine of scar tissue, the Sideways Lady had touched it. *I like shiny things.* Tess's heart thumped painfully as she recalled. The sensation of the creature's finger moved through her flesh. Stripping her identity. Claiming her.

32

The Matron

"I've spent hours in a dusty shop, fixated by gruesome things. Mum always said it was strange. Looks as though she was right," Tess said.

Dot's fingers fluttered, and Tess wondered if she'd once smoked.

"The books were there for a reason."

"You mean my nan?"

"She always thought it might be you. We all did because we tried so hard for it not to be." A surprising tear disappeared in the lines on Dot's face.

"What do you mean?"

Helga dabbed a crumpled tissue to her eyes and sniffed. "We sought her out. Aside from Mary, the three of us understood more than anyone what was happening Sideways. What *she* was capable of."

"Why did you try to talk me out of it, then? What was all that nonsense before?"

"We promised Charlie." Helga pursed thin lips, screwing up the tissue between ugly fingers.

"He's afraid for you, Tess, and we agreed. Of course, we did. He was desperate."

Tess smirked at Dot. "He won't be pleased, then."

"No."

"If it's the right time, right place, there's nothing we can do. Your nan always knew, and it was foolish of us to second guess your destiny."

The smirk wiped from Tess's face. "Don't say it's my destiny, Helga. Don't think I can bear it."

"We take one step at a time," Helga said.

"We?"

Dot tugged Tess's hands towards her. "We'll help you in any way we can."

An anxious knot tightened, and Tess pulled her hands back. Destiny still rang in her ears. *Right time, right place.* She'd been living a lie. Learning how to fix watches. Relishing gory details of a bygone era. All the while, Sideways lurked and the Sideways Lady waited. Tess thought of Rav. She longed to see him. To look into honey-flecked, soft brown eyes.

She sniffed a tear. So much for not showing weakness. "I'm not special or magic. I'm just me and she's … what is she?"

A memory of Alice stirred, her ghostly voice filling Tess's head, like a moth beating its dusty wings. *She takes everything you are. She takes your soul. Is what you fear and what you hate, and it's forever.*

"We have a theory." Helga opened the book of names. Tucked in the back was a yellowing envelope. With stiff fingers and knotted knuckles, she opened it, retrieved an old photograph, and pushed it across the table.

From sepia tones, a woman glared out, black eyes emotionless. She wore a stiff, white collar and a large cross, dark hair tied back from her broad flat face. She clutched a small bible, chest puffed out, lifted chin. Despite the godly effects, something about the woman's face sent a shiver of revulsion throughout Tess.

"I've seen her picture. I have this book—"

"She was Matron of Thorncross Asylum." Helga's strong German tone was low and full of hatred.

Dot stared at the picture. "Records portray her as an evil woman. Ruthless and greedy. She kept money donations, even those from Christian benefactors. After the fire, they found her surrounded by gold sovereigns."

I like shiny things. Tess's mouth was suddenly bone dry. "And that was just the beginning of Sideways?"

Dot replied. "In the ashes of the fire, Sideways grew roots. Running deep, spreading fast like black mould. Deadly."

"And the Matron's evil lingered on after she died. A slumbering monster, patient and intelligent." Helga's small eyes grew wide. Horror reflected in the blue.

Tess remembered what Grandad said. *A manifestation of madness, or evil.* "So, the Sideways Lady is a version of the Matron?"

Dot shrugged. "That's what we think. From what others have said, it makes the most sense, and there are very few who've lived to tell the tale ..." Dot hesitated, and Helga clutched her hand.

"There is a similarity," Helga murmured.

Tess's eyes lowered to the grainy picture. The creature she'd met wasn't human, but those black, soulless eyes and pasty flesh were the same. She turned the picture face down, wanting to block the image. Impossible.

"Like the Matron, she's greedy. Mad, we think. And brutal. Soulless and heartless." Dot's fingers fluttered to her chest.

"How do I stop her, then?"

Another uneasy silence descended. Tess waited, batting down the hatches beneath. They wouldn't know, of course. Why else would they be fidgeting, throwing glances towards each other? No one knew how to stop the thing that had once been the cruel Matron of Thorncross Asylum. No one knew, and only Tess would get the chance to try. It didn't matter that she didn't want to. Her destiny was fixed the moment *she* lured Teddy. Perhaps from the moment a young Knocker-Upper had woken up the slumbering monster. Barricade Street. The war medal. Tess was a soldier. *What was it Nan used to say?*

"We don't know how to stop her." Dot sounded weary. Helpless.

"*You* will find a way! You have this *connection*—"

"Helga, please don't say that," Tess snapped.

"It means you can win," Dot said.

"Precisely. Your nan was always so worried it would come to this, but somehow, she knew it would. She always said there was something different about you. *You shone.*"

Tess flinched at the choice of words.

"She was proud of you. Said you were braver than you realised. We believe that, too. You have this determination. I see it in the flash of your eyes."

"Thanks for the pep talk, Dot, but maybe if Nan had said something. Warned me."

Distraught, Helga leeched onto Tess's hands and gasped. "Don't think that. How could she warn you of this? You cannot tell someone their lives are blighted and expect them to enjoy the time they have."

The old woman withdrew her hands and hid her eyes with crumpled tissue. Tess pitied her. Helga was right, but if Tess had known, perhaps Teddy might never have gone Sideways. Perhaps stayed away from the clock shop. Chosen a different path. *The wrong path.*

Bone weary, Tess strolled to the picture window. Even the grey cobbles glimmered. She perched on the wide window ledge. "Helga, you said she can never pass to this side, didn't you?"

"Yes."

"But?"

Helga shredded tissue between her fingers. "Once upon a time, a Knocker-Upper woke the Sideways Lady. Years later, Tess of the Clock Shop opened the door."

"My trail."

Helga nodded, gloomy. "Don't fret. She may never be able to go beyond your grandad's shop."

Don't fret. Tess resisted the urge to laugh. "What will happen if no one stops her and Sideways keeps growing?"

Dot returned from the kitchen with a tray and three mugs of tea. "I have another theory."

Tess returned to her seat. "Go on."

"Have you heard of the Great Stink?"

"Yep. Victorian London at its finest. Open sewers. Sketchy sanitation."

"Did you know that Victorians believed the smell killed people?"

"Understandable."

Dot poured sparkling sugar crystals into her cup and stirred the muddy liquid with a bent spoon. "I think the Sideways stink *will* kill people because it's glutted with *her* stench. The stink of evil. At first, only the old or very young will suffocate. As for the rest of us, it will be a slow death. Passing through open windows and beneath doors. Blown on the wind." Dot clattered the spoon onto the tray. The little café fell silent.

Tess saw it all. Could smell it. She gripped the warm tea in her hands. She'd return to the clock shop. There, beyond the wooden gate, Sideways lapped against a concrete shore and the Sideways Lady lurked beneath the waves.

33

The Memory Bag

Helga shifted in her seat. She seemed nervous and glanced at Dot. "I have something that may help." She caressed the bag.

"Go on, Helga," Dot cajoled.

"I will read your bag, and before you say anything, I'm not mad."

"I didn't realise bag reading was a thing," Tess said.

Dot pulled a face. Half a smile. "It's Helga's thing, but it works."

Tess eyed Helga over the rim of her mug. "Okay. What do I have to do?"

"Nothing. Just believe."

"I'm not sure. Never been into psychics, or readings."

Helga pursed her lips. "And the Sideways Lady. Would you have believed in her before?"

How could Tess believe in something so monstrous? Even after seeing *her*, was she real? These two old women with a notebook full of names. The little café, once a blacksmiths. The clock shop and cobbled stones outside. Was any of it part of the real world?

Tess closed her eyes and listened to her ticking heart. A sound heralding her existence. She *had* to believe. Had no choice. She opened her eyes again. Both women stared, both uneasy. Tess offered a small smile. "Let's do it."

Helga pushed the bag across the table. It sighed open and tugged Tess towards the black hole of its gaping mouth.

"Not just a bag, you see," Dot said.

"No."

"Reach in, Tess. Your journey starts here."

Tess looked at Helga. The old woman leaned forward. Intent, eyes darker, face a mask. Tess had seen pity in those eyes. Now she saw something else.

A cold draught blew from the bag's depths. Tess had a feeling it held hidden things she didn't want to touch. "What will happen when I put my hand in?"

"It's unexpected," said Dot.

Tess drew the bag closer. The material rippled at her touch, icy fingers hovering over the opening.

"Reach in and ask for help. Memories in that bag long to be of service." Helga's tone was pious.

Suddenly, it was cold and silent. Was it Tess's imagination, or had it grown dark? She looked over her shoulder. The cobbles outside gleamed before. Now she couldn't make them out. *Had someone transported the little café?* An unwelcome tingle snuck upon her. *Had the bag swallowed them?* Nonsense, yet an unearthly stillness pervaded.

Tess turned back and saw magic dancing in Helga's grey eyes. She would believe because she felt overwhelmed there could be something more powerful than Sideways. She reached into the bag. The biting, icy abyss snatched at her fingers. Tess wanted to tug free, but the bag took hold. The chill swept up her arm, taking her breath.

"I have something." Tess jerked her arm free and held out an object. It clattered to the table.

"The dice," Dot said.

The dice refused to settle, dancing through spilt sugar diamonds. All eyes watched.

"What does it mean?" Tess asked.

"Shh!" Helga glared.

Making up its mind, the dice stopped spinning. Three black dots.

Helga muttered in German, then narrowed her eyes and hid the gleam of magic. "To the serious business. The bag will offer three objects, each one a weapon."

"A weapon?" Tess imagined a sword. *Was she capable of wielding one?*

"Not a sword or dagger!" Helga snapped.

"It will be unexpected," Dot said.

The bag numbed Tess's fingers, an unnatural chill snaking along her arm as she grappled with objects refusing capture. She held her hand open. Something drifted into her palm. Another old photograph faded to a bright yellow hue.

"Again," Helga barked.

Tess delved deeper. Something hard bumped her knuckles, and she grabbed it. *A tin of paint?* Tess placed it next to the photograph and opened her mouth to speak, but Helga stopped her. Goosebumps popped across Tess's body. The bag waited.

Tess reached in up to her shoulder, wondering if she'd have to climb in. There! She grasped the object, then placed the small cardboard envelope on the table. She fell back against the chair's uncomfortable wooden struts.

Darkness receded, and Helga tugged the bag towards her. When she looked at Tess, the magic had left her eyes. She was an old lady with silly hair.

Tess eyed the objects. "Now what?"

"I said it would be unexpected," Dot replied.

Tess picked up the small tin and read the label. *Silver Shine*. She prised open the lid. The pink sludge inside looked familiar. Smelled familiar. The cardboard envelope was an ancient book of matches, *The Gin Palace* scrawled across the shiny cover. Inside, one match stood to attention, its neighbours spent. The black head reminded Tess of a soldier's bearskin hat. She tossed the matches down, wondering how two old ladies duped her into believing something as absurd as a bag reading.

Dot stroked the book of matches. "From your pub, Helga. These are old."

"Years old."

Tess nudged the old photograph with her finger. "How will these things help me?" Expectant, she looked between the two women. Surely, they had answers. In the distance, the street seller called out again. Tess drummed impatient fingers against the table, hope fading like a wisp of smoke.

"The bag has given what you need," Helga said.

"Yes, but what am I supposed to do with these things?"

"It's not always clear," Dot said.

Tess spluttered, picking up the tin of Silver Shine. "Am I supposed to shine the Sideways Lady to death?"

Dot cringed. "We can't tell you what to do, no more than we can do it for you."

Tess scowled. "Right."

"The answers are there," Helga mumbled.

Tess gathered the objects and dropped them into a carrier bag. Wearily, she stood. "Nice to meet you."

Helga clutched Tess's hand. "We'll be watching for you. All three of us."

The magic in small grey eyes swirled briefly. Or was it a trick of the light? Helga was nothing but a mad old lady with a big bag. Tess withdrew her hand and edged towards the door, treading only on the white tiles of the monochrome floor. Irrational, but she was afraid to tumble through the emptiness of black squares.

The 'Open' sign scrawled in cursive red invited Tess Sideways. She tugged at the door and turned back to Dot and Helga, frozen in their seats. Both women's eyes followed her. Three empty mugs stood amid sugar sparkles. Tess pictured the ghost of Nan in the chair resting askew. She recalled something Nan used to say. *Those boots will march you right out of trouble.*

"See you again," Tess mumbled, turning away before either woman saw her crumpled face and tears snaking down her cheeks.

"Do you think we'll see her again?" Helga said.

"She has to believe in herself, and I don't think she's there yet."

"No. Not yet."

"And we're running out of time."

"Yes. I can smell that we are."

34

The Red Girl

Despite assuring Grandad she'd come straight home,
Tess had an intuitive urge to merge into the grey of
London streets. Part of her thought she might disappear,
not Sideways, but Victorian London perhaps, then she'd
be there at the beginning.

Tess's footsteps echoed out of time, as though
someone else walked and she was the shadow. She felt
disconnected but plodded along. Would keep going,
without looking back. Teddy popped into her mind. *How
easy would it be to renounce responsibility for him?
Could she reassure herself Grandad was right, and she
was putting herself and Teddy in harm's way?* A niggling
doubt told Tess not even Grandad believed it. He'd
enlisted Dot and Helga to convince her a fulfilling life
might be possible, but neither had. Those two old ladies
told her she was the only one who could stop the Sideways
Lady. Mary believed that too.

Bunching up her shoulders, Tess strode on. Why
should she believe them? Why even listen? She was
fifteen, her life ahead of her. She'd escape London. Try to
forget. Pretend if she had to. With every step, the pot of
silver polish banged against her leg.

She passed a man peddling tourist junk. Cheap
trinkets, flags, hats in red, white, and blue. He appeared

troubled and gazed at Tess as she neared his laden cart. With a jolt, she saw him for what he was. A man who'd been Sideways. No doubting the disquiet expression in his eyes. The exhausted slump of his body.

Tess waved, and a spark of light ignited him. "Hat, darling?" he chirped, thrusting a ridiculous top hat towards her. "Or flags. Buy two, get one free. How about a mug? Nice cuppa on a cold day." The man waved his flags. Hopeful.

"Sorry. I don't have any money."

The vacant expression returned. "Stop wasting my time, then."

Tess scurried away, merging into the damp London mist. Echoing footsteps were even more pronounced. She knew she should return to the clock shop, but London hadn't finished with her. It had a message, and she must listen.

Up ahead was a bridge, and she wanted to see the River Thames. London was built around the river, the heart of the city. She climbed narrow steps, hand brushing against ancient stone scarred with history. Beyond the wide wall, the water lay low, a muddy bank laid bare, revealing its sordid filth. The smell drifted towards her, a curdling mist suspended over the water. The bridge disappeared into hazy murk, thickening mist diluting the noise of traffic. For a moment, Tess was in another time. She closed her eyes, imagining what it had been like during the Great Stink. Poverty, overcrowding, people terrified by the terrible smell. And now the Sideways Lady was coming.

Tess heard a noise and opened her eyes. Along the wall, in the city's direction, uneven steps led down to the riverbank. In Grandad's day, moored boats, vital for the continued success of the British Empire, would've sat along the wall. Now, the steps served no purpose. Coated with stinking sludge, they led to the soup of the great river. No one in their right mind would want to step upon them. Unless drunk. Or a child …

Dressed in red, wearing black shiny shoes, a little girl made her way towards the grey paste of the riverbed. From the unsteady way she navigated every step, Tess guessed she was five—maybe six—years old.

"Look, Daddy. A shiny, silver fish!"

Tess could have been a bystander in a dream. The child's voice echoed, as Tess's footsteps had echoed. Her hair whipped in the wind, splaying it around innocent pink cheeks. She was smiling. Excited and eager. Without mercy, a grey beast would swallow her and one day, London would suffer the same fate. Scores of people living half-lives, never understanding why they felt less than whole. They'd be the lucky ones. There would be others who'd be *her* playthings. Perhaps this little girl.

London had shown Tess what she needed to see. With a racing heart, she stumbled along, never taking her eyes from the child. She heard the girl's dad calling out, forbidding her to go on. Saving her from Sideways.

"Your shoes will get dirty, Ava," he scolded, lifting the child into his arms. She saw Tess and waved with her little hand.

Tess didn't have the heart to wave back. She turned away, retracing footsteps, but instead of taking the short route past Dot's café, she walked along Dickens Row to Blackbird Lane, then turned left. The Old Gin Palace stood halfway down. Battered. Weary. Dot had mentioned three points of the triangle. The Last Stand. Sideways escaped where it could. Through cracks and tears, allowing it to trickle through, but there was an ocean behind the shop ready to swallow everything in its path if it broke free.

The picture on the sign above the pub—a green gin bottle—was the same as that on Tess's book of matches. It meant nothing, though it occurred to her drinking copious amounts of the stuff may well make everything disappear in a haze. She passed the pub. Muted chatter and laughter filtered through a closed door. Tess tried not to breathe in the heady odour of stale booze. She reached the corner of Barricade Street and headed back to Grandad's, passing drab doors and watchful windows. A street devoid of life. How had she never noticed before? How long had the narrow buildings stood quiet and empty? Once, a baker's shop stood there. *Was the aroma of baked bread clinging to the cobbles?* Tess passed an old ironmonger's shop, yellow lettering dull and peeling. She peered through a window. Save for a shroud of dust, nothing inside. Nothing but ghosts.

She looked up, but the blue was far away. Unreachable.

35

Glass Snowflake

The bell's happy jingle seemed obscene. Like breakfast. Like the sunny day.

Grandad sat at his table, wonderful hands immobile. He looked defeated. Deflated. "You're late," he choked.

"Always am."

Tess perched on a stool. On the table sat the Magic Drawer with its discarded treasures. She fiddled with a silver escape wheel.

Grandad watched. "They're like the socks of the clock industry. Always odd bits floating around."

"A bit like Helga's bag."

"Pardon?"

Items glittered at Tess. She selected a broken loupe. An intricate snowflake splintered into one lens, making it useless. "Never mind."

"I called your mum and you're going home tomorrow."

Tess resisted the knee-jerk reaction to protest. She held tight to the loupe. What good would it do to tell this wonderful man what she knew? "Okay." She kept her eyes lowered.

"You understand, don't you? Why you must leave? Why I asked for Dot's help to discourage you?"

"I understand, Grandad."

"I can't risk losing you, my dear."

Tess ignored the break in his voice. She stood, still clutching the loupe. "Can I borrow this?"

"Keep it."

How old he looked. And tired. How much more pain would she revisit upon him? Tess climbed the mountain of stairs, her mind in chaos. One moment resolved to accepting her fate, the next fighting against it. She kept arriving at the same crossroads, but one thing was certain. Her life was no longer her own.

She settled at the kitchen table and lined up the objects taken from Helga's bag. She opened the lid of the silver polish and recognised the odour from a forgotten memory. She studied the book of matches. Inside, outside, back and front. At one time, there must have been twenty or more matches lined up. Little soldiers in bearskin hats.

Tess tucked the matches away and stared at the photograph. Difficult to make out the features of the wide-eyed child staring at her, and yet, the face wasn't unfamiliar. She flipped the picture over. No markings, no date. Hunching over the table, she nestled the broken loupe against her eye. Her thumb knuckle rested against her cheek as Grandad had shown her.

The glass snowflake shattered the picture's pale face, the eyes splintering Tess's soul. The girl had fair hair hanging to her shoulders. It was obvious from her clothes and the dingy background she wasn't from a wealthy family, though far from a slum child. At least she wore shoes, and those eyes, full of hope, or so Tess imagined. She was from working-class London. Another world to one Tess knew where children had to work. Where a seven-year-old boy may have been a chimney sweep, or a little girl, a Knocker-Upper.

Tess's heart clamoured in her chest. Hand shaking, she put down the loupe and stared at the picture. The girl stared back. Plucked from the depths of Helga's Memory

Bag, a picture of Alice. The child, a little older than the red girl, almost lost to the swampy Thames. Could it be an elaborate trick? Perhaps. But why? Tess fought rising emotion. Guilt. Frustration. Fear. She'd wanted to forget Alice. Had desperately tried to ignore her plight.

She peered out from her world to the one beyond. Even the little courtyard was no more than a grainy image seen through dirt-speckled glass. A grey box with an orange ball and green jerry can. Then, beyond the gate, the wilderness of Sideways. Suffocating swathes of metal coloured nothing. A tread on the stair alerted Tess. She tucked the photograph away, then yanked opened the door under the sink. Next to furniture polish stood another tin of silver shine. That was the familiar smell. As a child, she and Nan polished trinkets until they gleamed. A distraction might be useful. Tess took the medal from her pocket and sat down with her tin. She was ready with a smile when Grandad emerged around the doorframe. His troubled gaze eased when he saw her.

"Thought it was high time for a sort out," he said, placing the Magic Drawer on the table.

"I'm hoping I can make this medal shine."

The old man clutched the edge of a chair. "I've shut up shop. The princess will pick up her watch tomorrow, and I don't expect more customers today."

"You okay?" *Stupid question.*

"Think I may need to sell the shop."

"No! You can't. It's been in your family for years. Besides, it's what I want to do too."

"What good is this shop when that's out there?" Grandad wandered to the window, clinging to the sill like a desperate man.

"Grandad—"

"I'll sell and live with you. Your mum won't mind."

Neither of them mentioned Ivor.

Tess sighed. "Even if you do sell, Sideways won't go away."

"For us it will. If we leave, we can live normal lives. Forget all this."

Tess heard the hope in his voice but couldn't ignore the conflict in his eyes. She pressed her forehead to the glass. "Pretend it doesn't exist, you mean?"

"Exactly!"

Tess had to tell Grandad everything. His age and the lines on his face proved his strength, not his weakness. "What happens when someone else takes this place over? A property developer would demolish it and build flats here. We can't let that happen, can we? *I can't let that happen.*"

"Don't see we have much choice."

"I'm not so sure. Turns out, Nan chose her friends well. Thanks to Dot and Helga, I know about the Last Stand."

A horrified mask slipped into place. "What?"

Despite everything, Tess grinned. "Don't blame them, Grandad. They tried."

"It's not your job. Not you. Not my granddaughter ..." he choked on his words, fumbling for a handkerchief to dab at his tears.

"What would Nan say, I wonder?" Tess fought the tide of emotion struggling with the anguish in old eyes.

She glanced around the kitchen, once full of cooking smells and sweet-smelling freesia. Nan's presence lingered still. Her bone china cup, a favourite pen she used for crosswords. One day the dust would win, but not yet. Memories stirred. Tess pictured her sitting ramrod straight, intelligent eyes appraising. Had she always known this day would come?

Grandad's desperate voice broke through Tess's reverie. "No! We leave here. Right now."

Tess's gaze fell upon the medal sitting on the table. A medal of bravery belonging to her great-great-grandfather. "We can't leave our post."

Grandad's face crumpled. "That's what your nan would have said." He didn't look at Tess again. Proud and brave, fists clenched by his side, he turned and left the room.

36

Stars

How quickly life changed. In a heartbeat. The tick of a clock. One moment, Tess embraced it with confidence. Now, the illogical and inexplicable tarnished the vision of a well-defined future.

She thought of Rav, the boy with pearl-white teeth and melted chocolate eyes. He'd be waiting for her. *He* was part of her future. College, too. Holidays to Spain. Australia, one day. Now? Biting back a despairing groan, Tess focused on the food congealing before her. *Was this her last supper?* The knife and fork chinking against crockery set her teeth on edge. Grandad toyed with his food too, trying to prod a lump of sausage to life.

Tess gave up and scooped her leftovers into a food bin next to the window. She watched peas make a dash for freedom and roll across the windowsill. She saw the orange ball outside and a multicoloured memory appeared.

"Grandad, how long since you sold Amber?"

"A few years now. Once your nan died, I had no need for a car."

Tess thought of Ivor's statement car. Pristine interior, sleek lines, and sickly smelling tree hanging from the rear-view mirror.

"I used to love going for drives in that car. I remember the noise of the engine. Magical."

"I let you drive it once. In the country somewhere. Your mum told me off." The old man chuckled.

"I remember."

"I could have given it to you."

Tess closed her eyes, trying to blot out the sound of the pain-filled voice. Behind her, she heard a chair creak. A sniffle.

"Tess …"

"Time for a cuppa, Grandad. Go and sit down and I'll bring one in."

Only when she was alone in the kitchen, hands in hot, soapy water, did Tess allow herself to feel the fear that tainted every movement. Every breath. Cold dread she thought she'd drown in. To lose herself in happy memories again, she dragged her mind back to Amber, the orange car, but memories faded, and the car lost its colour. Everything dulled and slowed. Tess imagined she stood in the storm's eye, where everything was still and eerily peaceful. Keeping her company was the terrible knowledge that at any moment it would pick her up and spit her out. That she'd be a tiny speck in the middle of maddening chaos lingering like white noise from an out of tune radio.

After Grandad went to bed, Tess shined the war medal, then polished the old and rusting watch parts from the drawer. A ceramic dish held all the useless treasures Teddy had gathered. Old picture hooks, nails, springs. She polished them too, all the while wondering about *Charles Smith, Lieutenant.* She muttered to him, willing him to join her ranks.

When the wall clock ticked past 11pm, Tess knew it was time. She wouldn't sleep. Didn't want to sleep. What was the point of twisting and turning for hours? Seeing Grandad again? Having him wave her off? It would likely break him. Far better to leave now, while something that might be courage stirred inside.

Tess crept downstairs into the shop. She listened to the clamour of clocks. Smelled the smells that once meant refuge. In the gloomy kitchen, she eased back the bolt that now yielded into its bracket. Grandad must have oiled it. Tess took a breath and yanked open the door. A full moon illuminated the sad little courtyard and bathed it in a silver glow. Stars scattered the night, filling her mind.

For a moment, standing in the glow, Tess imagined the universe was on her side, but the moon and stars blinked off, blotted out by the growing swell of Sideways. She cursed the universe and padded across the courtyard. Through the gate, into the wilderness.

37

Moon Face

An ocean of stinking grey swallowed Tess. She focused on the monolithic monster of the ruined institution. Her beacon. Smelly Mary and Alice would know what to do, but she doubted she'd ever reach them. The Sideways Lady lurked. Tess could *feel* her. Could *smell* her.

Doubts flooded back, eroding hope and courage. She almost fell, breath catching as the cold and smell filled her lungs. Then a sound from the depths of the ocean. A gleeful gurgle. Laughter.

"Have you come to play?"

Tess may as well have been blind. *She* was everywhere. Snagged within the folds of her grey cloak, Tess grew weak. The cloak filled Tess's mouth, wrapping around her until she could no longer move. Pinning her arms to her sides. Jamming her legs together. A bitter wind swirled, tossing Tess like a dead leaf caught in a whirlpool.

Shame and despair flooded Tess's senses. She'd failed. Be lost forever. Seeing Teddy's splintered soul, Tess felt a stab of agony. *How would he survive without her? And what of Grandad?* Lost too, as grief consumed him. Wind howled, biting at her flesh. A hungry wolf ready to pounce. She would close her eyes, accept her fate, and it would all be over. She could sleep. Only a nightmare awaited. One from which she'd never wake. *She couldn't give in. Not yet.*

The medal was heavy against her numb scar, reminding Tess of who she was, what she was capable of. She was a fighter. Stronger than she imagined. Stronger than the Sideways Lady believed. Her mind rallied, but her body was weak. The tentacles of Sideways couldn't hold her, but Tess grew disoriented and sensed the creature trying to climb inside her body. Wanting to invade her skin. Infest her mind. Instinctively, Tess knew if that happened, she'd be nothing more than a plaything. *Her pet.*

With everything she had, Tess resisted, screaming with the effort of keeping herself whole and human. The Sideways Lady screamed back, her wash of stink flowing over Tess. Tess closed her eyes against the onslaught, a chill clinging to her like a fever. She wasn't sure how much longer she'd remember who she was.

Then a voice whispered. "Don't let her take you."

Alice. The little girl's pale eyes reflected her terror. The Sideways Lady rampaged with unpredictable fury, yet Alice had found the courage to seek Tess.

The creature growled. "I'm awake and I will take …"

"We need to get back to the fire," Tess panted, clinging to the sight of Alice. A little angel in the middle of stupefying carnage.

A moon face appeared out of the grey. Puffy and white, empty black button eyes. Bowing over Tess, lips rotted black, the fiend crooned in her ear. "Tess is mine, and we will play. Every night and every day."

Tess reached out, but she was underwater. Fighting for breath, flailing with desperate strokes.

Joyful, the Sideways Lady swirled about, then a sudden silence descended as the strange world held its breath. "This will be fun," she taunted, then disappeared.

Like steam from a cooking pot, her smell lingered, reminding Tess of the meat stew. She whimpered, fighting the urge to vomit.

"You came back," Alice said.

"I came back."

Tess's body convulsed as sweat pearled across her forehead. Her insides tightened. Gagging, she doubled over. Alice rubbed Tess's back, soothing her with gentle caresses and whispered reassurances that almost made Tess smile. Alice shuffled in the dirt. Little feet, the colour of the ground. Cold ash. Tess regained her composure, battling her body's weakness.

Alice led Tess through the unchanging desert. Footsteps muffled in the silent world.

Mary waited, hunched beyond the fire in the building's shadow. "You came back then." There was no mistaking the haughty tone. She spat into the fire, making it hiss.

Feeling like a schoolgirl, Tess disturbed the blackened bricks at her feet.

Alice shivered, drawing close to the flames. "Aren't you cold?"

"Yes." Tess took a cautious step towards the fire. "Sorry it took me so long to come back."

Mary glowered. Tess flushed.

"It wasn't time before." Alice jangled the watch on her wrist.

"Don't you want to come closer to the fire?" The old woman fixed Tess with an icy stare.

Mary was nearly invisible among her rags. Except for unblinking, staring eyes, reminding Tess of a wise owl. She heaved to her feet and hobbled around the fire. Tess stepped back, but Mary had business with her.

"D'you know why she thinks you're the same?" Mary jabbed a gnarled finger at Tess's chest.

"She said it was because we're different. And lonely."

Mary jabbed again. "What else?"

The fire crackled. Tess glanced at the flames. "Fire. We're both afraid."

Mary leaned in and peered into the depths of Tess's soul. "Time to stop doubting yourself. She's got inside your 'ead. Twisting your thoughts and making you doubt, but if you've listened to them that knows, you knows too."

"Making me doubt?" Tess choked, half laughing. How could she have imagined she ever stood a chance? The moon face would haunt her dreams forever.

Mary prodded Tess's chest. "In there, you knows."

Tess swallowed down the angry retort. What did Mary know? Wasn't she just another silly old lady filling her head with nonsense? She couldn't beat evil. Even with a sword! She swore under her breath as Mary hobbled away.

Plopping onto her well-worn seat of stone, Mary cackled. "Fine language for a lady. And you're right. You couldn't beat 'er with a sword."

"Get out of my head!" Tess knew Mary would ignore her, but what did it matter? At least with her, she didn't feel like a broken part of a whole. Tess gazed into the empty void of Mary's home—Alice's home—and pictured Samuel abandoned in the dirt. "There's nothing out there. Where *is* everyone? Where are all the ..." Tess faltered. *Did she want to think about countless lost children?*

Ancient and withered, Mary suddenly looked tired. How long had she been witness to the despair Sideways brought? Tess felt a pang of sympathy for the battered old woman, recognised the sorrow in narrowed eyes, the lives lost in every line etched upon her ruined face. "Them that fall asleep, like Alice, get caught in a snag. Your own little piece of Sideways. Unchanging. Wandering alone, 'til the dust claims you."

"What about the others? Those that don't fall asleep." *What about Teddy?*

Mary's mouth twitched. An all-knowing smirk that made her even uglier. "Once you go Sideways, there'll always be a part of your soul captured, but some can do without it. Maybe your Teddy is lucky, 'e might not need the part Sideways kept."

"What if he does need it?"

Mary huddled in her stone nest, casting herself in shadow. "Then he'll live 'alf a life."

Tess felt damp with fear and dread. What sort of life was half a life? She thought she'd saved him, but it might all be for nothing. *Half a life*. Tess grasped the idea, but it was like reaching for fog. "He might never be what he's supposed to be. Might never aspire to anything. Like Grandad's friend. Dead at forty."

"There are others," Mary muttered.

Despite the crackle of flames, the silence grew. Tess could hear pity in the rasping voice. She shielded her eyes from the fire's glow, but it was useless. The flames were too bright, and Mary's face remained hidden.

"Who else, Mary?"

"You already know." The silence roared. "Your mum."

38

Pyramid of Bone

Mary was speaking still, but Tess couldn't hear. Weak and dizzy, she staggered and reached out to steady herself. She clung to a metal skeleton. *Part of the roof, maybe?*

"You're wrong." Tess heard the childish appeal in her words.

Mary jabbed at the ground with her stick. "Don't tell me you didn't know!"

The metal bones had ragged teeth and tore at the flesh on Tess's hand. The pain eased the anguish in her mind. A part of her *had* known, but she'd refused to believe. Even when she saw Helga's book. There had to be more than one Jodie Smith in London.

Tess closed her eyes, replaying the conversation they'd had in the early hours. The look on Mum's face. Her trembling hands. The truth was crushing yet explained so much. Why Mum was never content. Why she never finished college. Never aspired to be anything, do anything. Jodie Smith had never been the person she was supposed to be.

Every night, sometimes until dawn, knitting, food, the blather of TV, all to reclaim the missing part, but Jodie Smith was half-empty and always would be. After the accident, she'd clung to her guilt. Wore it like a suit of armour. She relied on it and, in doing so, failed to let anything else in. Eventually, Jodie drove her husband away. Alienated her daughter. Then Ivor came along. He'd always held a torch for his old school friend, and when the time came, was content with half a wife living half a life.

Tess blinked back tears, releasing her grip on the metal. She felt the sticky damp of blood but didn't care. She may never see Mum again and so wanted to. To say sorry. Tell her how much she loved her. The bleak wasteland compressed her; a terrible weight she couldn't lift on her own.

"Why are you afraid of fire?" Alice asked, breaking the spell.

Tess eyed the sultry flames. Magnificent, yet deadly. "I was hurt a long time ago."

Tess traced the flesh of her neck. With splayed fingers, she could replicate the shape of the scar. Like licks from the fire. A brand. That was why Grandad called her a phoenix. Born from the flames. Tess hated her fear of fire because it made her feel unworthy.

She stared ahead, watching the memory unfold like a child's crumpled drawing. "I was about five years old. Dad built a fire so we could toast marshmallows …"

Tess remembered a neighbour calling over the fence, offering Dad mulled wine. He'd glanced at Tess as he accepted. *Don't get too close to the fire!* A beautiful spark rose into the black night, a soaring gold star spiralling downwards. Wanting to catch the falling star, Tess reached out, tottering towards it. She didn't see the flames. Couldn't hear the hungry growl. During the painful days that followed, screams would waken Tess. But not her own. They were Dad's screams. Meanwhile, Mum … *Mum.* Tess covered her face. She couldn't cry because she wouldn't stop. She took a breath and buried the terrible truth.

"It made you what you are," Mary snapped.

Tess eyed the old woman, unsure whether she meant the accident or Mum's half-life. Perhaps it was both. *Who was this ancient hag who understood things about her?* "What makes you who you are, Mary?"

The old crone cackled. "Likely when I was left on the steps of a workhouse and decided not to die."

"How can you decide not to die?"

"Didn't you do that, too?"

The heat from the flames warmed Tess. She didn't feel afraid. All-knowing, Mary saw too and smirked.

Tess did the same. "How can you ... how can *we* move backwards and forwards, between Sideways and the real world?"

"All my life, I wandered the streets of London. Knows every sound. Every stink. I sat right there, just about where you are and *felt* Sideways growing, trying to take me, but I knows myself too well and smelled what it was."

"A lie."

Mary pummelled her stick into the dry ground. "A lie. A trick. Dreams for the deluded."

"What about *her*?"

"A lie. A trick. Dreams for the deluded. As for 'er ..." Mary's grip tightened on her stick. "Even when she slept, she smelled when people came. That's why she wanted to be waked so bad. Why she lured the child."

Tess looked at Alice, who stared into the flames and clung to her legs. Bony knees, and too-wide eyes. Bound to the Sideways Lady since the day she woke her. How often had Alice blamed herself for everything that came after?

"It's been a long journey for me, but I knew I'd be here, at the end." Mary sounded defeated.

Tess studied her. An old, shrivelled apple. "How old are you?"

"As you know, Sideways time moves different. I'm no age."

Ruined teeth, deep crags upon her face, colourless hair and knotted knuckles all suggested Mary was a great age. Tess considered the possibility she'd been born that way. Delivered into the stinking river wearing the armour of age and dirt, claimed by stacked houses and cobbled streets. Fading eyes twinkled, or perhaps it was the firelight.

"What about Alice? You said if you fall asleep, you're alone forever."

Mary spat into the fire again. "Alice was from my time, and I watched Sideways carefully. I knew 'er and when I knew she went Sideways, I found 'er."

"And you stayed?"

Mary shrugged inside her rags. Her sacrifice had been easy.

Tess edged around the fire towards Alice. With her back to the institution, Sideways gaped with dizzying emptiness. An infinite space. A black hole. Breathless, Tess looked away. The fire crackled on. They were all just waiting, but for what?

"Sideways shouldn't exist," Tess whispered.

Mary pointed to the institution with her stick. "That's at the 'eart of it. All those tortured souls, eaten up with despair and madness. They've never known peace."

"What does *she* do if she catches you?" Tess regretted the question, but it was too late. An image came to mind. Her mouth. Slab of tongue. Cherrystone teeth grinding on metal.

"She likes to eat you."

A little bird's chirp. Or had Tess imagined it? Alice stared. Pale. Doll like.

Tess gulped, heart racing. "What did you say?"

"I think it's quite quick," Alice whispered.

Alice's pale eyes gave nothing away, and Tess had an urge to reach out and shake her.

"Show 'er," Mary barked.

Alice seized Tess's hand, the chill of little fingers sending an icy ripple along Tess's arm to her heart. She dragged Tess past the menacing metal to the exposed side of the institution. Under their feet, bones of the building crumbled to dust.

"There," Alice pointed.

A pyramid, crudely constructed from bits of the devastated building. Shards of stone and metal entwined—a macabre piece of modern art—but something else, too. Tess stepped closer. Another step, another, then she saw. Hundreds of jutting, white bones. A foot, a pointing finger, mad staring pits in hollow skulls. Tess gasped, wanting to unsee, but unable to tear her eyes away. Mary embraced her as she stumbled.

"She eats some, while they still 'ave their colour. Makes 'er stronger. Their minds make 'er clever. That's why those others are lucky. They escape and live 'alf a life. Always 'ere, always there, but never suffering this fate." She kicked at a bone. It clattered to the foot of the pyramid.

The skulls' staring eyes fixed upon Tess. She withdrew further, turning her ankle on rubble, and looked down. Not rubble, but bone, with a flag of faded red, wilted in the dry dirt.

39

Right Place, Right Time

Tess couldn't breathe. Couldn't bear the horror. Bolting from the bone pyramid, she climbed over the rubble to the graveyard of a garden, where the remains of a wrought iron fence stood. She sat on a low wall. A faceless stone demon that was once a smiling cherub kept her company. Tess smelled Mary before she saw her.

"If I stop her, there'll be no more bones?" Tess watched a strange Sideways bug burrowing into its dusty home.

"No more bones."

"And Sideways will be what it always was? A wrongly taken path. A distraction."

"Yes, but …"

Tess narrowed her eyes. "What?"

"It won't be an easy victory."

"Impossible, you mean."

"If you're already defeated, no point in fighting."

Every scrap of energy left Tess's body. She felt the Sideways poison fill her veins and soul. "When I left Grandad's, I was ready to believe this was my destiny. Now I think it's madness. That I don't belong."

"You and I both knows that you won't live any sort of life if you leave 'ere now."

Tess didn't want to listen anymore. Wanted to put her hands over her ears and blot out anything else Mary had to say. *Just a silly old lady.* Except Tess didn't believe that. Perhaps it was the wisdom in Mary's eyes. As fixed as her stink.

Mary tilted her face skywards. For the briefest second, she appeared young. A beautiful woman with eyes lifted to heaven. The fire cast a golden glow on her features, erasing lines, making her flesh shine. "I hear 'em. Scores of lost souls. See 'em sometimes too. The little girl who dropped that teddy bear. People are weak, y'see, and Sideways *entices*, promising something different, but it's all in the 'ead. I've seen so many folk lose themselves. They feel the world owes them. Don't make that mistake." Mary threw Tess a disparaging look. Once more, a shrivelled old hag.

Tess clutched her chest. "I never expected anything from anyone. I've lived with this, the pain, and the scarring, and because of it, am the person I'm supposed to be."

"I don't doubt that, Tess of the Clock Shop, but sometimes you have to stop and listen."

"There's too much noise out there," Tess muttered.

"I mean, you have to listen to what's *inside.*"

Why did Mary have to make sense? Tess turned her back. She sat frozen, afraid, but a little voice reminded her she could still see Grandad's gate from the corner of her eye.

Mary grimaced, revealing little nubs of teeth. "Don't ignore where your path has led you and think you can choose better. That you'll be happier if you go another way. Because you'll live only 'alf a life and will always, *always* regret. Do you understand? *This* is your destiny. Right place. Right time." Mary eased to her feet. Her gaze cruel, cold.

A freezing wave of understanding crashed over Tess, filling her with the dreadful truth. Everything she knew washed away, leaving a discarded shell on a shore of blackened bones. But Mary wasn't done with her yet.

"Your doubts, guilt, and sense of injustice have deserted you now, thankfully. Don't let 'em back in. You need to invite courage in. And strength. And cunning. You need to start believing."

"That's what Dot and Helga said."

"Acceptance of what you are is one thing but knowing how you fit into the world means the world's no longer a mystery and anything's possible." Mary hobbled away, leaving Tess alone in the strange twilight.

The dust bug reappeared from its hole and scurried along a narrow, well-worn track. What purpose could this creature serve in such a barren place? As though pondering the question, the bug paused, probing the air with fine antennae. Then it froze, so camouflaged that it almost disappeared. Tess stared until she wondered if she'd imagined the creature. Then it jumped, ensnaring smaller prey, before dashing back home.

Cocooned in a grey blanket, Alice tiptoed through the gates. Perhaps sensing despair, the little girl placed the blanket around Tess's shoulders, perched beside her, and hugged bird legs into her body. Leaning her head against Tess's shoulder, Alice hummed quietly and lay a gentle hand on Tess's leg.

"Mary said this was your fate, but I wouldn't blame you if you went home. I would if I could."

Alice was a version of the dust bug. A creature that had carved out an existence, evolving into something colourless. Yet here she was, offering comfort. What could Tess give back?

"Tell me how you became a Knocker-Upper, Alice. Tell me about your London."

Alice stared into the cavity surrounding them. "I was ten when Granny Edith gave me her bamboo pea-shooter. She showed me how to tilt the shooter, how important it was to puff just the right amount of breath."

"Must have been hard work—"

An expression of joy passed across Alice's features. "Oh, I didn't mind. I *loved* London early in the morning when it was still dark. Quiet and mysterious. I'd imagine another life, where I was a proper lady with fine clothes and dancing."

Alice sniffled, hugging herself tighter. "Mary explained something once. She used the word covet. She said it was wanting something that doesn't belong to you. When you want something so bad, you forget who you are. She told me even things like the fleas and Da's drinking were part of my story. An important part that would've made me a better person. Braver. Stronger."

Tess recognised the aged wisdom in the pale glint of Alice's eyes. "I think you're the bravest person I know."

"I was happy, too. Trouble is, I forgot who Alice was and strolled off my path. That's when Sideways got inside."

"Didn't you *smell* it?" Tess remembered when she'd first stepped Sideways. The odour dismantled her senses. Like being bulldozed.

"No smell. I had this feeling inside, like a warm flame. Everything felt just right. Perfect even. My shoes weren't too small, I wasn't so hungry, and then …"

"Then?" Tess pressed.

"I knew I had to wake something up. Then the smell comes for you. Alive! A monster made up of smell."

Pain, both mental and physical, had been the foundations on which Tess flourished. In the cruelty of a fiery embrace and a brand upon her flesh, Tess discovered who she was. She'd never felt envious of unblemished flesh, and when other people were uneasy because of it, she was sorry for them. Every look, every comment, made her stronger.

Sideways changed everything. Alice's ghostly shape, the joyless sound of her voice, was a different kind of pain. "Do you remember your family?"

Another smile split Alice's face. "I had a baby brother. Samuel."

Tess recalled Alice's gentle touch and soothing words when the Sideways Lady had left her shaking and sick. "I bet he loved his big sister."

"They'd all be dead now. Even Samuel. And that makes me sadder than anything because I'm still here." A sob escaped, but Alice bunched her shoulders, clenching hands into fists. "I wish …"

Tess prompted with a gentle touch. "What do you wish?"

"My sister Mollie was older than me, but she was scared of monsters hiding under the bed. Mama told her if she went to sleep, she'd dream, and monsters weren't allowed in dreams." Alice's face crumpled. "I wish Mama hadn't told her that because that's what I did. When no one could see me, I fell asleep in Mama's bed. When I waked up, I was here, with *her*. Stuck forever."

An unbearable silence followed, but Tess's mind raced. *There can never be another Alice.* Tess jumped to her feet and pulled Alice with her. She snatched up the blanket, draped it around Alice's bony shoulders, and tied a crude knot at the neck.

"The Lady Alice." Tess bowed, taking the girl5 in her arms and spinning her around, making grey eyes sparkle. Suddenly, in that dead garden, laughter rang out and Tess felt a little less lost. A little less alone.

40

What If?

Tess stood before Thorncross Asylum, gazing up at the window. *Her* window. A monster's bird's-eye view. It had taken Alice three peas. Three peas to wake a beast.

That fateful night, when flames speared the sky, the dark had grown a monster. Perhaps it heard the screams, smelled the burning flesh. Maybe *felt* the scorching heat consuming the Matron. The skeleton of the institution was scarred, its soul defiled, yet, within the walls, a scent of hope. Except one room, where an evil essence lurked. Where *she* belonged. What if Tess could make the creature go back to sleep?

She watched the flames as they danced. Lighting up their dark corner. Throwing malformed shadows against stone and dirt. A plan formed, and the fire gave it life.

Mary nestled in her nook. "You plan on returning." It wasn't a question, so Tess didn't answer.

The old woman sucked in her breath. "If you return, you'll be weakened, distracted, but I see you must."

"It's the only way."

The grey of Sideways thickened, black streaks swirling, whipping up layers of dust. A storm approached.

Propelled by renewed urgency, Tess followed the well-worn path. Clock parts strewn across dirt trampled underfoot. Distracting herself as she ran, she called out the names. Faithful boots carried her, a soldier on patrol. In the time it took Tess to reach the familiar back gate, stillness had settled upon her. She nurtured the feeling. She was Tess of the Clock Shop and could do anything. Panting, she halted, calm dissipating in a clock tick. Resolution all but forgotten.

Buffered either side by empty buildings, the narrow shop blazed with light. Why wasn't it dark? Asleep? Tess hurtled through the gate and paused at the back door. *What was the noise coming from within? Was Grandad in danger?* Cautiously, she pushed open the back door and stepped into fog. The kettle sang, steam spiralling from its spout. Tess switched it off and froze at the clatter and mumbled voices. She crept towards the internal door, peering through rippled glass panels.

She pushed the door wide. A whirlwind had ripped through the shop, leaving a trail of disaster. Loitering in the middle of the debris stood Dot and Helga. When they saw Tess, both gasped. Helga clutched parts of the ancient cuckoo clock that belonged on the wall. Dot held the splintered back of a chair.

"Hello. You're back," Dot said.

Tess stared at the destruction. Smashed cabinets. Destroyed expensive sale stock. The faithful bell bent beyond repair. Books thrown from the shelves or shredded and scattered to the floor, her blue chair spewing its stuffing, gouged as though a wild animal had clawed through the fabric. Tess lurched further into the shop. An unmistakable aroma filled her lungs.

She turned to Helga. "Is Grandad okay?"

"Yes, my dear." Helga hugged the broken cuckoo clock to her breast. Her eyes flicked towards Dot and back to Tess.

"You were Sideways. Are *you* okay?" Dot said.

Tess nodded. She'd returned for a reason, but hardly remembered now. Exhaustion stole over her. She pictured her bed. The warmth of blankets. She could sleep for eternity.

Helga stepped forward. "Why are you back?"

Tess scowled. Helga was even smaller than she thought. Barely reached her chin. What right did she have to question her? "I forgot something."

Tess didn't care if she sounded rude. She turned to the stairs, then faltered. Had the creature been up there too? Destroying Grandad's home. Ripping up memories of his life with Nan. Tess chomped down on the inside of her cheek and tasted blood. She'd see for herself, then sleep.

"Don't go up there!" In pink, fluffy slippers, Helga tore across the shop and stood in front of Tess. "She's trying to distract you. She knows you're a worthy adversary, and she's scared."

Tess narrowed her eyes. "You've never seen her, have you?"

Helga stammered, her grip tightening on the cuckoo clock.

Dot planted herself next to her friend. "Helga's right, Tess. The Sideways Lady is scared but knows she can distract you with this." She gestured to the room, wielding the sword of splintered wood.

Tess sneered. "*This is Grandad's home.*"

"Yes, and he's fine. You mustn't forget your—"

"My what, Helga? My *destiny*?"

Helga frowned. "Faith in yourself. You felt it. I know you did."

"Please, leave. Both of you."

Helga grew in stature. "Don't stop believing. You *can* beat her."

"How do you know? Did your bag tell you?" Tess stifled a laugh but saw a flash in Helga's grey eyes.

"*Dummkopf! Warum glaubst du nicht?* Why do you not believe?" Helga's disdain was clear. "Ja, my bag told me. All day I have spent reading the bag."

Dot touched Helga's arm, but Helga turned away, muttering. "Der hohlkopf! Hollow head."

"She's frustrated, Tess. You're so close now. We both feel it."

"Close to what? Getting my insides sucked out, or whatever it is she does to people."

Wearily, Tess shook her head. When was it she believed she had a chance? Was it only moments ago? Looking down at her dusty boots, at the devastation in the shop, everything had changed. She was free of Sideways. Home. What if she ignored them all? Crawled to bed and slept. Alice would become a distant memory. She deserved to live a normal life, didn't she? A headache formed. Tess screwed her eyes shut.

"Where's Grandad?"

"I'm here."

The sight of him filled Tess's heart. What would she do if something happened to him? He plodded downstairs. The familiar creaking sounded monstrous. Old bones. Old house. Tess licked dry lips. Her head pounded.

With a fleeting touch, Grandad stroked Tess's cheek, then went to his broken worktable. The only thing in one piece was his chair. Helga helped right it, then he collapsed into it.

"She's destroyed everything, Grandad."

He waved his hand. "All *stuff,* Tess. Replaceable. She can't hurt me. Not here."

"Upstairs?"

He shook his head and gripped both knees, but it didn't stop them from twitching. Tess glanced up the narrow staircase. Her face bathed in the landing light's warm glow and eased her troubled mind. It would be easy to forget now. One step, then another.

A loud crack echoed. Tess spun around. In trembling hands, Helga had snapped another piece of the cuckoo clock. She spluttered, dismayed.

"I think you've broken it," Grandad chuckled, surprising them all. Then he looked at Tess and drew a weary breath, clinging to his knees like a man clinging to a life raft.

"You can go home, Tess, but I don't see what good it will do, long term."

"I didn't think you wanted me to fight this fight!"

Grandad released his knees, peering at Tess from beneath untamed eyebrows. He massaged his scalp, giving him the look of a mad professor. He wiped his face, big shoulders heaving.

Tess went to him and dropped to her knees, wrapping her arms around his waist. She felt the scratch of his old jumper. "It's okay," she murmured.

He held her shoulders. "It's not okay. None of it is, but I now believe, perhaps always have, that you must face *her*."

"Lucky me."

Frail and dishevelled, the old man plucked Tess's hand, massaging it in his own. He whispered to her, blue eyes flashing. "*She* doesn't stand a chance."

Tess untucked the medal from beneath her jumper. "Do you think I'm worthy?"

Grandad slowly shook his head, face lined with grief. "You don't need a medal, not when your heart and soul are full of fire."

Tess touched the star, warm against her fingertips. She felt nothing. Grandad was right. She didn't need it. The medal was a lump of metal, nothing more. She tucked it out of sight and climbed to her feet. She felt taller. Despite the wobble of fear in Grandad's voice, he believed in her and his belief meant everything.

41

A Galaxy of Time

Dot and Helga crept about the shop, moving aside broken bits of furniture. Awkward fingers gathered up pieces of clock and laid them on the gouged work desk. Most pieces ruined beyond repair.

Tess swept up glass, watching silver streaks of dawn from the front window. She ignored the uneasy pitter-patter of her heart. Not so easy to ignore were the troubled glances coming her way.

"It's not fair to leave all this to you."

"It just gives *her* more time," Dot ventured.

Helga's limp candyfloss hair waved in agreement. "Perhaps, it's time to say goodbye to your grandad. Not goodbye! I didn't mean …" she whimpered.

Tess let the broom clatter to the ground. "Fine." She stomped up the stairs. Fraught whispers rose and followed her ascent.

In the kitchen, the kettle shrieked to silence. On the table, where Grandad had left it, sat the Magic Drawer. *Was it only last night?* Tess peered in, wondering over how many years the Smith horologists had acquired the hodgepodge of precious time artefacts. She stirred the contents with her finger, as Grandad often did. From a dusty corner, a diamond winked. Mesmerised, Tess grappled in the dust and held up the gem. What good was a diamond's sparkle? She let it fall and leaned against the window. Her destiny was out there, shrouded in grey, looking more like her grave than her future.

Grandad was beside her. Enjoying the comfort of his presence, Tess listened to him breathe, feeling weirdly calm. When she looked, the old face was alight, and she saw a kaleidoscope of memories dancing before his eyes.

"Since you asked about the car, I've been thinking about all those lovely trips we went on when you were little. All those picnics. The beach. You had terrible procedures to endure but were always determined never to let anything get you down. You were resilient. Such a fighter."

Tears sprang into the old man's eyes, and his lips quivered.

Smiling, Tess nudged him. "I loved my time with you and Nan. That little car was more magical than Chitty Chitty Bang Bang. One minute we were in the middle of London, the next, the middle of nowhere. Nan used to pack *everything*, didn't she? I mean, no matter what, the car had supplies for any disaster."

"Always prepared, your nan."

Tess stared at the green can in the courtyard. "Do you remember the time we broke down? We were in the middle of nowhere with no phone, just us three."

Grandad winked. "She planned that. Thought 'breaking down' might make it more of an adventure."

"Really? I remember writing a story about it for school."

"We loved every minute we had with you and were proud to be your grandparents."

Tess felt his arm heavy about her shoulders and the squeeze of fingers into her flesh. It felt as if the old man were saying goodbye and somehow, that was okay. She gazed around the little yellow kitchen. Thought of the shop that had stayed unchanged for years. A place caught in time. The same dust swirling about. Same creak of old boards. The cobbled street outside, once overrun by plague, and burning beneath a great fire. If she didn't face the Sideways Lady, her life would be on hold, too. A stopped clock.

"Time to go," she mumbled.

Grandad poured cooled water into two mugs. The Magic Drawer sat in the middle of the table. Despite dusty corners, the diamond shone. Though small, other objects glittered silver and gold. Even Teddy's worthless collection of screws and nails—now polished to a high shine—looked as though they belonged.

Tess gazed into the drawer. A galaxy of time. The tiniest gasket. A miniature star. "Grandad, what if the contents of this drawer really are magic?"

"There's nothing more magical, nor mysterious, than time."

"Can I take all of this? I mean, you may not get it back."

"Whatever you need." Grandad stirred his tea, focusing on the whirlpool inside his cup.

Tess scooped up handfuls of treasure and buried it in the pouch of her jumper. She took a breath, held it, then let the air trickle free. There was nothing more to say. Steadfastly, she marched from the kitchen. Tess thought she heard Grandad call her name, but couldn't be sure, and couldn't go back.

Downstairs, Dot and Helga muttered back and forth. Anxious looks. Scared, staring eyes. Helga still clutched the cuckoo clock. *Would the shattered pieces end up in the bottom of her memory bag?*

"I'm leaving."

"Now?" Dot stepped towards Tess.

"No time like the present."

Helga hugged the clock parts tighter. "Oh, dear. Oh, my dear. You are so brave."

"Not a dummkopf, then? Not much choice, have I? You both made that clear." Tess enjoyed the pink blush on Helga's cheeks.

"Come back to your grandad, Tess." There was an urgent appeal in Dot's voice.

Helga reached out a hand, bejewelled fingers gently stroking Dot's. Dot had lost someone Sideways.

"I'll do what I can."

"Just believe," Helga said.

Tess turned away and walked through the shop as she had a thousand times. She paused in the courtyard, the eyes of the house behind her, and understood this may be the last time she saw it. Time had irrevocably arrived and Tess of the Clock Shop, the horologist's granddaughter, was the one to bring an end to the Sideways Lady's reign. She was ready as she'd ever be.

She picked up the old green can, surprised at its weight but relieved too. Who needed a sword?

42

Warrior Tess

Stepping Sideways, Tess left behind her old self, and a new self, Warrior Tess, walked in her boots. The bitter chill of Sideways quenched her bones and powered her steps, but not for long. Relentless, icy fingers suffocated and snagged her throat. The institution had never felt so far away.

In the glare of her flames, Mary waited. "Wasn't sure you'd come back again."

Tess grunted in reply. Weakened, she fell into a stone seat and basked in the fire's glow, trying to coax warmth back into fingers and toes. "Where's Alice?" she asked, voice hoarse.

Mary gestured to the institution.

"And where is *she*?"

"'Ere or there."

"Definitely not 'ere," Tess muttered. She couldn't smell her, just the fetid aroma of the Sideways stew.

"No, but she'll be back."

"I was hoping she might be gone forever."

Mary squinted at Tess. "She'll keep you waiting if she wants to. Do you have a plan?"

"Sort of."

Mary spat. "Sort of might not be good enough."

"No."

"Don't underestimate 'er."

Tess leaned forward and peered at Mary. "I won't, but she's underestimated me and you."

A gust of wind blew across the fire, making Mary's rags billow about her. An unpleasant smell reached Tess. Not Mary's smell. A warning.

"I'll be back." Tess stood.

Mary pointed with her crooked finger. "What's that you're hiding?"

"Modern magic," Tess said.

"Careful, you don't burn yourself."

Was Mary inside her head again, privy to her thoughts and plans? Accepting, Tess turned to face the institution. How still everything was. How quiet. She took a steadying breath. Time to complete her mission.

Tess navigated steps shifting under her weight and let a trickle of treasures fall, making the stone glisten. Gold and silver sparkles to dazzle and entice. Shadows swallowed her as she crossed the threshold into a world of whispering ghosts. She'd explored the institution with Alice, but this time was different. Tess felt vulnerable. *Would the ghosts want to keep her?* She peered into the dark corners, flesh prickling. Perhaps they were waiting for her.

Tess touched hand to brick. *I want to make things right.* Her fingers tingled. The asylum listened. She crossed the entry hall and imagined the women's fear when they heard the Matron's footfall and jangle of her keys. Did they plead with her, or suffer in silence? Tess flinched as she pictured the cudgel landing heavy blows on soft flesh. The Matron's violence would leave marks beyond the physical. Madness on madness, seeping through the stained stone of their cells.

Then the fire happened. Tess stared into the gloomy void. She could *feel* the anger, but ghosts couldn't hurt her, could they? She descended into the tomb. Despite the intense heat of the fire, the metal door remained intact. For over a century, it had stood sentinel. Helpless women not overcome by smoke would have died slowly. Starving and desperate, their cries unheard or ignored. The door had no reason to buckle now, and that didn't feel right. The fire had to reach every dark corner.

Tess leaned her shoulder into the cold metal until it shifted, scraping and scratching against stone. A hungry tide surged towards her. Dismembered souls reaching out, wanting to claim her. She tried to tell them she would send their tormentor back to sleep, but frigid air snatched her breath. Tess closed her eyes and waited.

In the end, she needed no words. Stillness settled in the ebb of darkness, the prospect of peace simmering in the gloom. They trusted her. Tess turned away. She wouldn't fail them as once they were failed.

43

A Million Wings

Though fearful, Tess no longer doubted she was in the right place at the right time. That feeling ran through her veins. Clamoured in her ticking heart.

In sturdy boots, she climbed the remains of the sweeping stairs, pausing at the summit to listen. A scratching noise. *Rats?* No. Not rats. *Children.* Whispering now. A fleeting movement. She'd disturbed their game. In the middle of the hallway, an abandoned black metal pram frame. Inside, swaddled in a filthy blanket, a bald wooden doll with black dots for eyes, and a red painted mouth. The doll stared at Tess. She didn't like dolls and pushed the pram away, but the wheels buckled, and it squeaked to a stop. Rueful, the doll stared out.

Glad to turn away, Tess went to the dormitory and found Alice cross-legged on the floor. The teddy bear sat at her side. Despite his missing eye and matted fur, he looked friendlier than the doll. Alice scratched crude pictures into the stone floor, clutching a piece of chalk as white as her hand. The tip of her tongue poked through pale lips.

"I like your flower," Tess said.

Alice scribbled the petals white. "Mr Smith had flowers in his front garden."

"Mr Smith?"

Alice glanced up. "He saw me before Sideways took my colour away, then sent Mary. He had a clock shop. A real gentleman he was."

Could Alice be talking about Tess's great-great-grandfather? Tess stared through the postage-stamp window. Between black bars, to the grey. All those years ago and here she was, perhaps only a little younger than he'd been when he first went to war. Now she had her own army gathering, willing her on.

Tess squatted down to watch Alice draw. A big oval with white stripes and wings.

"Is it a bee?"

"Don't remember." Alice dropped the chalk and rubbed her hands together. Chalk dust drifted down like bonfire ash.

Tess tugged the medal from round her neck. In the morbid light of the asylum, the star dazzled. She'd made it shine. She placed the medal around Alice's neck, its green ribbon stark against ivory flesh. Everything in the little girl's world was bleak. Slate sky and pictures drawn with white chalk. Even Samuel. The worn teddy was as grey as the stone floor where he lay, his frayed red ribbon blotched with dirt.

The medal made Alice's eyes shine.

"It's a medal for bravery, and now belongs to you."

Alice turned the medal over in her hands. "What do the words mean?"

"It's the name and rank of someone who fought in the war. Lieutenant Smith. Charles Smith. I think he was your Mr Smith's son. My great-grandad. Perhaps you even knew him?" Tess let the words sink in.

"Charlie Smith! All the girls liked him before he went off to school, but I was gone before the war. Mary told me all about him. How he lost a leg."

For a moment, Alice disappeared, her face crumpled in concentration. When she spoke, her voice was that of an old woman's. A life lived long ago with only dusty memories remaining. "A red rose grew near the door and there was a gold number four."

Could it be the same metal number, now tarnished and dull? "Number four Barricade Street," Tess murmured.

"And Charlie's eyes were bright blue. Like ... like—"

"Like the sky on a bright day."

Alice gripped the medal and stared from the prison window. "Like the day the king was crowned! There was a street party with toffee apples—" Alice choked, silver tears spilling from her eyes. Perfect raindrops.

"I'm sorry, Alice. I didn't mean—"

"Don't be sorry. You've helped me remember who I was before Sideways."

Tess opened her arms and Alice filled the space. She leaned her head against Tess's heart as though listening to its rhythm. Tess's tears fell steady, pain chipping away at her soul. There was a strange peace as they huddled together, then fingers of cold crept through the window bars.

"I'm laying a trap," Tess said. She stood, feeling empty without Alice to hold.

"What kind of trap?"

"Come and see." Tess took Alice's hand and led her from the dormitory. At the top of the stairs, she pointed.

Alice gasped at the glittering trail.

Tess delved into her pocket and handed Alice more of the treasure. "She likes shiny things and if we can get her back to her room ..." Tess stopped, her throat suddenly dry.

"What will happen then?" Alice placed a silver spring on the ground.

"Magic mixed with fire to send her back to sleep."

A good plan in theory, but a lot could go wrong. Tess shrugged off her doubts. Failure was impossible. Unthinkable.

They laid a trail to the office, the room where evil still lingered. Simmering darkly in corners. Where the Matron invited depravity into her soul. Where hopefully, it would all end.

Self-belief fluttered inside. Tess entered the room, the remaining treasure spilling through her fingers. She tore down the strip of black fabric at the window, smoothed it flat upon the blistered windowsill, then placed the diamond in the centre. She stood back. *Would the Sideways Lady enter her tomb for this tiny gem?*

Tess turned to face the shadows. "I'm sending her back to you. Make sure you keep her this time."

Alice watched warily from the doorway, but the shadows stayed silent. Outside, the Sideways stew bubbled. Tess knew she'd done all she could. She marched from the room and dashed down the crumbling steps.

"Get Samuel and wait for me," she called to Alice.

Mary sat on her stone throne outside the asylum. She grasped her stick like a staff, a wire crown of thin, frizzy hair on her head. "Bravery don't always mean fighting. Being brave is knowing when to let things run their natural course. Knowing when to walk away."

Surely she didn't mean to chip away at Tess's self-belief? Tess edged around the fire until she could look into troubled eyes. "Do you always have to be so cryptic, Mary?"

The old woman chewed on leather lips. "Just saying."

Tess clenched her fists and inhaled deeply. "I'm making this up as I go along, so, anytime you want to tell me what you think I should do, feel free."

Regal, Mary gazed into the fire. Something remained unsaid, but Tess knew Mary too well. The old woman wouldn't spare her. She waited. Inside, a million wings fluttered.

"This, right 'ere, is the right path for us. You and me."

"I know, that's why …"

The old woman reached out, clutching hold of Tess's arm, and stopping her. They locked eyes and Tess felt a sudden chill.

"Still possible to stumble from your path," Mary hissed.

Tess looked down at the charred fingers. Felt them digging into her flesh. She tried to pull away, but Mary was strong.

"The Sideways Lady don't 'ave a soul, but you do and 'ave to listen to it. Above all, be brave. When the time comes, be brave! Remember, sacrifice is never easy."

Tess stumbled backwards, yanking free from Mary's clutch. "What are you saying?"

Mary hunkered deeper into filthy rags. "She'll be 'ere soon enough."

The queen of dirt and fire was right. Sideways was stirring. A mournful wailing from the bowels of a grey monster.

Tess's heart skipped. "Am I going to die, Mary?" she stammered, words catching in her throat.

Mary sighed. A deep, sorrowful sound. How frail she looked. "Do you really believe your life 'as led you to this moment? That this unspeakable horror is your destiny?"

The wind blew stronger. Tess imagined a pack of wolves racing towards her, relentless in their quest. Time was running out. She traced the raised area of her scar. The brand on her flesh meant she could never forget who she was, but she was lucky. She liked the person born from the fire that day.

More than anything, Tess wanted to live, but her path had led her Sideways. She was where she was meant to be. Mary prodded the fire, eyes fixed on Tess. Inside the girl's head again, the old woman nodded. "Well, then."

Tess picked up her green can. "Thank you."

"What for?"

"For looking after Alice. For not letting me forget about her."

Mary grunted in reply, but as she turned away, Tess glimpsed a hint of a smile on the grizzled face.

"One more thing, Mary. Don't let the fire go out."

The thought of dying terrified Tess but spending eternity in Sideways was worse. She would win or die trying. She squared her shoulders and faced the asylum. Besides, Mary may be wrong. She still had a plan and would follow it through. If that didn't work, another plan might come. If not. *If not ...*

Tess ascended the steps. From the can, she drizzled petrol, coating the shining treasures. Inside, she splashed more over crumbling walls and the chewed up remains of the old, wooden desk. She doused the steps leading towards the locked cells. *No mistakes this time.* Tess followed the trail of shining crumbs to the first floor and looked down the broken staircase to the front door left open in invitation. *Follow the breadcrumbs. Come inside where you belong. Sleep.* Tess smirked. *And they all lived happily ever after.*

The can was lighter now, but there'd be enough.

"Thanks, Nan," Tess mumbled.

Organised and always prepared. Picnic blanket. Water. Map. And a green jerry can full of petrol. Just in case. After his wife died, Grandad sold the car, but before the buyer came to collect it, he moved an orange ball and green can to the back garden. From that day, he'd barely given the items a thought.

Tess hadn't either, until she kicked the orange ball, and it bounced off the green can full of magic.

44

A Desert Twilight

Tess covered everything in petrol. The metal pram frame. Piles of rotting blankets. The wooden doll would burn too. *Alice's home*. A familiar prick of guilt caused her to falter, but the child was turning to dust. She'd have no need for her sad little bed and stained, crispy blankets.

Samuel lay discarded on the floor. Tess stooped to pick him up, the chalk flowers and little bee smudged underfoot. No matter. Tess fled from the room, away from the sad drawings, from the tangle of blankets and the wooden doll. Trembling, she clutched the doorframe and stumbled past the stairway. Along the landing, blackened with soot and dirt, glittering now. Black snow.

At the office doorway, the petrol ran out. Alice sat in the middle of the floor. Small, and silent as a little mouse.

Tess stepped over the threshold. "Alice? I found Samuel."

With a half-hearted smile, Alice turned. Puffy eyes. Tears shining silver against her marble face.

Not happily ever after, after all.

Tess sat and bopped Alice on the head with Samuel. It would do no good for her to break down again. She sat the bear in Alice's lap and waited. Hands shaking, Alice held out a sepia photo with curled edges. Tess plucked the picture from her grasp.

"I know it's not Mama. This place burned before I was born, but it looks like her. What if Mama ended up in a place like this because she never found me? What if all this time, thinking she growed old and had grandbabies to cuddle, she never did? Maybe she died suffering? Did my brothers and sister die too? Baby Samuel?" Alice buried her face into the bear's matted fur, shoulders heaving.

Tess reached out. A gentle touch, but Alice cried harder, the heartbreak overpowering. Even shadows shrank in their corners.

"They tortured ladies here. I know because sometimes, at night, I can hear their screams."

Tess flinched. Alice's tormented life curdled her blood. She'd read enough literature to know Alice was right. Victorian asylums were unspeakably cruel places. Torture for treatment. Electric shocks and cold baths. Isolation chambers. Desperate women in straitjackets or chains.

Alice glanced around the room. "I was always afraid to come in here. Not just because this was where *she* was before I waked her, but because of that."

She motioned to the buckled filing cabinet lying on its side. Contents spewed from yawning drawers. Most of the files had burned to ash, but among the ruins, black eyes, white faces, and scattered words. Alice scrambled to her feet, clutching Samuel, damp with her tears and more forlorn than ever. She gazed from the small window.

"We're going to make that lady in the picture peaceful, Alice. We'll burn this place down and give her and the other women peace. Okay?"

"Not for me." Alice's voice was barely audible.

Tess closed her eyes and drew a breath. She felt ready to fight. To face the Sideways Lady and accept her fate. If she died—unthinkable—but her boots and the invisible army standing at her side made her believe. Gave hope. What did Alice have? What formed her world? A battered old bear and a room full of ghosts. Anguish stalked her like a shadow. Tess joined Alice at the window. Their bodies touched and Tess jerked. The little ghost at her side. Cold and empty.

Wide, pale fixed eyes on Tess. "When this is over and you go, it will just be me and Mary again. Forever and ever."

Tess focused on the barren wilderness, pain carving her heart. If she could fly, she would soar far away, but only if Alice could too. The fact she never could, left Tess with a hole inside, as bleak and chilled as Sideways. But Tess could still think in colour. She could hear birds, the sound of waves crashing. If she closed her eyes, she could see stars. But Alice had nothing. Not even hope.

Tess dug chewed fingernails into her flesh. Her wound reopened, and she felt sharp pain. She didn't care. Was glad for the hurt.

"Nothing is forever, Alice. Even stars die."

"Really?"

"They burn to ash. Gone. That's how time works. One minute there. The next, gone."

Alice stroked the medal around her neck. "I can't imagine this star ever turning to ash."

The silver of Nan's slender watch caught Tess's eye. "One day, I'm going to be a horologist. That means I know how time works. An oscillator counts every second. That's what makes time pass. One day, like the star burning out, the oscillator stops working."

"And then time stops?"

Tess needed Alice to believe. *She needed to believe.* Nothing mattered if Alice had eternity to endure.

"Then it stops."

The little girl clutched the medal and stared out. "What's a hologist?"

Tess laughed. "A horologist is someone who knows about watches and clocks. Like Mr Smith. In fact, now I think about it, time worked out perfectly. It brought me here. To you."

"Your destiny?"

"Exactly. Now, don't forget you're my lieutenant right now, and I need you to help me defeat the enemy," Tess smiled.

Alice pushed out her chest and lifted her chin. "Can we really beat her?"

"I think we can."

The contours of Alice's face softened, a small smile splaying across her mouth. Tess recognised hope.

"We're going to tell the children." Alice marched from the office. Samuel, dangling from her fingertips. The bear peered at Tess, his one eye accusing.

A feeling of horror circled Tess's mind. A cluster of feasting vultures coming at her from dark corners. 'Liar, liar,' they squawked, but she batted them away. Hope endured when there was nothing else.

Outside, Sideways changed. A storm of churning grey clouds in a desert twilight. A tornado, and the asylum standing in its path. Time to focus.

Tess hurtled from the room, leaving a single bloodied handprint against the glass. "She's coming, Alice!"

Alice ran from the dormitory wearing a coat far too small. Red, but blotched with dirt and mould. A crash shook the building, and she stumbled. Tess caught her, reaching out to steady herself against an unsteady wall. Another booming crash like an immense wave hammering the building.

"Stay close!" Navigating chunks of stone, Tess flew down the stairs, dragging Alice behind her.

Another boom and from upstairs, something heavy crashing to the floor. Tess thought it could be the dormitory ceiling. If the savage weather destroyed the institution, there'd be no chance of tricking *her* back inside.

They reached the doorway. Ripped from its hinges, the door lay several feet away. Sideways swirled and frothed, spinning around the asylum. Tess clung to Alice, frightened the wind might pick the little girl up and carry her away. Amid the pounding squall, laughter vibrated. Tess closed her eyes. She would ignore the stench that tried to fill her up. Fight the fear that threatened to drop her to her knees. She had to stand strong. *Believe.*

"Take the medal back," Alice shrieked.

The two girls locked eyes. Tess smiled down. She didn't need the medal. She edged towards the slurry of Sideways. "I'm not afraid of you!"

The wind swallowed her words. The laughter grew shrill. Tess trod upon the next step. One way or another, her journey would be over soon, and she had no desire to die. She relished the sensation of her ticking heart. Heard its steady rhythm louder than the storm. Felt it stronger than fear.

Suddenly, all grew still and quiet.

Tess squeezed Alice's hand. "Your mama wasn't mad, Alice. When she lost you, she was sad, but she would have carried on loving your brothers and sister. She didn't end up somewhere like this, I promise."

Giving someone hope was never a bad thing.

"I'm scared," Alice whispered.

"Me, too."

A voice ripped through the grey. Vicious claws. "I wonder why Tess wanted Mary to keep the fire burning. I asked, but Mary wouldn't say. *Had to punish Mary.*"

"Where is she?" Tess resisted from calling Mary's name. She couldn't die! Not when she was as ancient as London streets. She'd found somewhere to hide.

A grim silence settled. Any moment, the creature's face would appear. Bloated and pale. Tess scanned the empty grey and waited.

"Has she gone?" Alice whispered.

"No."

There was a whooshing sound as though something was gathering up Sideways and from within the folds, Mary. *Not Mary.*

Like aged fruit, the old woman's tiny, shrivelled frame floated above them. Her stinking rags hung loose, and unmistakable pale eyes stared unseeing. Mary was dead.

45

Lieutenant

The corpse drifted down and jerked towards Tess, creaking with every monstrous step. From inside Mary's body, the Sideways Lady leered. "What have you done, Tess of the Clock Shop? For years, I left the old hag alone. The girl, too. Then you came along and changed the rules."

The blood in Tess's veins ran with ice. The creature spoke the truth. Tess clenched her fists. *Why had Mary trusted her? Why had any of them believed in her?*

Only Alice kept Tess on her feet, injustice for the child sparking within, but it wouldn't be enough. Not without Mary.

"Why did you have to kill her?" Tess said. Despite the tremors in her body, her voice never wavered.

Purple lips parted, showing the blackened stumps of Mary's teeth. "She had too much to say for herself so, I silenced her. Not before I picked through her mind and saw what you meant to do to me."

"I don't know what you mean."

Darkness glittered behind the sheen of Mary's dead eyes. "You meant to send the flames after me. To swallow me. Burn me up like they did my Matron. Well, my poor, disillusioned Tess, the fire's gone and Mary is dead. Time for you and me to have some fun."

"I won't be your pet."

An icy finger traced a pattern around Tess's face. "I admire your bravery. Foolish, of course."

The creature swooped away, swallowed by folds of grey. Then, from nowhere, a sickening thud as rags plummeted to the ground. *Mary.* The old body lay broken beyond repair. Tess crouched over, unashamed of her tears. Peaceful in death, vacant eyes stared.

"She's dead, isn't she?"

Tess climbed to her feet and ached for the child standing lost in her little red coat. "I'm sorry."

Alice whimpered, shivering as the biting wind howled. Suddenly, the earth shifted. Blackened rubble, like pieces of bone, danced in the dirt. *Was this what an earthquake felt like?* The ground gaped and sent Tess sprawling. For a moment, she disappeared. The cold, the stench, Mary's dead body, all faded to nothing. Tess turned her face. *Rav.* A breath of warmth tickled her flesh.

Rav's eyes shone as he leaned towards her. "Tess." He reached out, breathing deeply and entwined his fingers with hers.

A dream. Snatched before she lived it. Sideways dragged Tess back. She lay near the gaping wound in the earth. It stretched wider, mocking her.

Alice called her name. Tess blinked, vision blurring. Like an old snapshot, a little grey girl stood motionless before the asylum, arm outstretched. Dangling from her fingers, a shiny medal attached to a vibrant ribbon.

The Sideways Lady prowled, gaping at the shining star. Any moment now, she'd lunge at Alice. Tess groaned and got to her knees. She heard a voice and turned. Mary's dead eyes stared out. *Had she spoken?* Impossible, but then Mary defied time and, more than once, had climbed inside Tess's mind. Was she trying to guide her?

"Tell me, Mary."

The Sideways Lady howled. "You seek counsel from a corpse?"

Tess crawled closer to Mary, but death held the old woman.

"Don't leave me, Mary." Tess closed her eyes and replayed the moments that brought her to this point. How could she defeat this creature without Mary and her fire? She tumbled backwards in her mind. Grasping, grasping, the way she'd grappled for objects inside Helga's bag.

Helga's bag. The match.

Tess opened her eyes. Mary stared. *Careful not to burn yourself.* The old woman knew, but the battle was over, wasn't it?

The bait unseen, untouched. Hope scattered in the icy wind, yet something had changed. Face transformed, Alice stood on the steps of the asylum, the ghostly pallor replaced with a pink flush and a peculiar smile meeting her eyes. She held herself rigid. A lieutenant facing down the enemy. Then, she spoke.

"You think you're the mistress of Sideways, but *I am.*"

"Child, beware." The creature stood frozen.

"Time is controlled by this star, with the oscillator inside, and you can't take it from me because you're too afraid." Alice took a step.

"Wait! Explain what you mean."

"I can split this star and take the oscillator out. Sideways disappears. *You* disappear." What was Alice doing? Tess thought about leaping over the chasm, but the Sideways Lady stood transfixed. She'd wait a moment. Bide her time.

"Nothing can stop *me.*"

Alice swung the star. "You're wrong."

Panic rose, choking Tess. Now she understood what Mary meant. Being brave and making sacrifices. *No. Not Alice. Not after everything she'd endured.*

Angered, Tess glanced at the old woman, but the peace in fading eyes defied her. If Alice died, she'd be at peace, too, but Tess couldn't bear it. "Alice!"

Alice fixed her gaze on Tess. Impossible to conceive, but she looked happy. "Right place. Right Time."

The little girl disappeared inside the asylum. Furious, the Sideways Lady shrieked, yet still she faltered, afraid of going back into her tomb. She crouched low and caught something glinting from the stone step. A jewel. *She liked shiny things.* In the asylum, shadows gathered and waited in welcome.

Unsteady, Tess got to her feet, throat aching with the effort of holding back sobs. The mournful wind wailed. The creature edged closer to the asylum, the glittering path proving too much temptation. She'd follow it and snatch the star before the child could do anything. What did *she* have to fear? Black eyes swivelled towards Tess. *You have nowhere to run.*

Tess held the terrible gaze. Understood the unspoken message but felt no fear. The wind ceased moaning, Sideways fell silent again, and the Sideways Lady turned back to her path and disappeared inside. Tess crumpled to the ground, no longer able to hold back sobs. How could she light a flame and burn down what was left of the asylum with Alice inside? She pictured the girl in her little red coat. A child-ghost. Braver than Tess could be.

She looked at Mary. Was she really dead? "Why didn't you tell me? Why did you make me think it was me? I could bear that. Not this. Not Alice!"

Did you notice her eyes? Tess started. Not Mary's voice inside her head, but her own. *Did you see Alice's eyes?* Bright blue. A summer's day. Peaceful.

Tess stood and dragged her arm across her face, smearing tears in the dirt. She leapt over the gaping chasm and beheld the grey expanse of Sideways. She had the sensation of being in the middle of a vast ocean, waves rolling far above her head, never crashing down. Distant land forever hidden. No gate on the horizon.

Inside the asylum, the darkness held its silence. Tess reached into her pocket and took out the cardboard book. Alice had been brave. She must be braver. Give the little girl her peace but suffer a lifetime alone. That would be her sacrifice. Inside the little book, one match. Tess tugged it free. She closed her eyes, prayed, then struck. A bright flame danced on her fingertips. She released the match and watched a trickle of fire follow the shiny trail.

At first, it looked as though the flames would have no impact on steadfast stone walls. That the dark might snuff the fire out. Instead, shadows danced, whipping up flames. The trickle became a stream, then a raging river. Tess backed away as the fire roared. Heat seared her flesh. No one would survive. Plumes of smoke set sail in the ocean of Sideways. Spirits trapped for years soared into the grey and disappeared. Free as birds. Alice would soar too, flying high, at last. Tess heard The Sideways Lady's lament. A long, drawn-out cry. Then silence and calm.

Long ago, when intelligent minds thought the devil wore the mask of mental illness, the asylum was built. Brick by brick, a bleak prison rose, tainting the land forever. For over a century, tortured, desperate souls left their imprint. Then a fire burned, fanning the flames of evil.

Lost to time, Tess watched the building collapse. A fallen monster. Flames died. Evil snuffed out. The Sideways Lady vanquished.

Tess walked among the ruins. Close to the remains of the steps, Samuel lay on the ground. "I'll look after him for you," she cried, gathering him up and holding tight. The little bear brought comfort. There was nothing else.

46

A Flame

In Tess's ticking heart, time passed. Moments undefined by light or dark. In the graveyard of rubble, she explored. Some things were too terrible to behold. An ugly doll had defied the flames and only partially burned away. Charred edges of red fabric. The twisted frame of a metal bed.

Something glimmered. Tess clawed among the building's charred bones to free the shining object. Once in her grasp, she sat on a slab of stone and held it for a long time. The war medal, its inscription, no longer decipherable, the green ribbon, long gone. Tess decided to leave the medal among the ruins. For Alice. A final resting place.

For her? It would be easy to give up. Perhaps it was inevitable, snagged as she was within this forever hell. Tess sensed herself fading into the dust of her environment. She spied the colourless bug searching with renewed vigour. It stopped to pause, feeling the air. Tess reached out. The creature fled, but something else caught her eye and her breath. *A member of Alice's stone family.* She looked closer. A web of scars gouged into the neck, an impression of boots on the feet and legs. Recognising herself, Tess clutched the whittled figure, and shed fresh tears.

She stared at the bleak terrain. Deep, black veins scarred the landscape. Gaping arteries created by the storm and splitting in different directions, each pulsed with the stink of Sideways, spreading as far as the eye could see. The decision to leave the security of the asylum wasn't easy, but Tess knew if she waited, she might wait forever. She'd follow the widest rift and if it led nowhere, would follow another. She was a warrior. A phoenix. She was Tess of the Clock Shop. Could be anything she wanted.

Often collapsing with exhaustion, or sick with the overpowering stench, Tess never stopped searching for home. When the shadow of weakness appeared, she imagined Rav. His eyes. His touch. She breathed deep, remembering the smell of hot chips, now and then, glimpsing something twinkling in the dust. A tiny gasket. A spring. A golden escape wheel.

A flame of hope flickered inside. Growing. Glowing. Embracing Tess in its warmth. She smiled. *How ironic. A flame keeping me alive.*

ABOUT THE AUTHOR

Sarah J Maxwell loves literature. At 31, she received a first-class degree in English with Creative Writing. Leaving her stress in London in 2018, she moved to Tasmania and found her writer's voice. Sarah's reading choice is mainly YA fantasy, but she'll pick up any recommended book. When not writing or reading, Sarah walks her dogs, Bob and Fred, claiming inspiration ignites while traipsing through the Australian Bush. She has a passion for her craft and writes every day.

Sarah's other love is theatre. Over the years, she's acted in several plays. Her claim to fame is sharing membership of the same theatre company with Jude Law, who she saw on stage in a production of Laurie Lee's *Cider with Rosie*.

Friends, family, and cups of tea are Sarah's priorities. She's also partial to a gin and tonic, chocolate, and cake.

www.sarahjmaxwell.com

If you enjoyed *What the Knocker-Upper Woke Up*, the author would appreciate a quick review on Amazon, Goodreads, or your favourite book website. Reviews are vital. A few words matter.

ALSO BY SARAH J MAXWELL

Billy Lemonade
(Whisper Publishing 2021)

Available from Amazon
in paperback or Kindle format.

BILLY LEMONADE

Released worldwide on 20 January 2021

When a broken-hearted girl befriends a poor boy, the secrets haunting them may tear them apart …

Jane Smith is too lonely for words. Ignored by her grieving mother, uncaring teachers, and peers, the distraught thirteen-year-old can't find any solace after the deaths of her father and sister. Resigned to an empty, isolated existence, Jane can hardly believe her luck when she meets a poor, older boy. Taunted, scorned, and stuck with a despised nickname, he's happy to be her friend.

Sensing the boy identifies with her pain, Jane finds hope as their friendship deepens over drifting summer days. But, when she suspects he's hiding a terrible truth, Jane fears deep secrets will pull them both back into the dark.

Will Jane make the ultimate sacrifice, release despair, and take them to a together forever place?

Billy Lemonade is a beautifully crafted standalone YA story. If you like real, raw characters, authentic drama, and a dash of supernatural suspense, then you'll love Sarah J Maxwell's unforgettable journey.

Available from Amazon in paperback or Kindle format.

ALSO BY WHISPER PUBLISHING

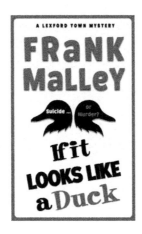

Released worldwide on 25 August 2022

A dead landlord. A suicide note. A man called Crime. And a determined reporter who's sure not all's what it seems.

When the body of landlord Roger Mansell is found in the River Lex, and a note uncovered on his boat, police say suicide.

Jaz Sharkey, a tenacious reporter on a failing newspaper, thinks murder. "If it looks like a duck, swims like a duck, and quacks like a duck, well …"

Her suspicions fence a bunch of regulars from the charming village pub. Identical twins, the psychotic ex of Jaz's mouthy sidekick, Trish Parker, and a man called Crime.

As Jaz and Trish look for clues and editor Dan Armitage fights to keep his paper afloat, things turn sinister.

Quirky and funny, but with all the pace, twists, and adventure of a mystery. Join the hunt in this arresting cosy crime.

Available from Amazon in paperback or Kindle format.

ALSO BY WHISPER PUBLISHING

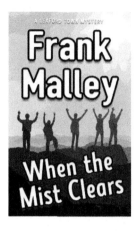

Released worldwide on 15 May 2020

One former war correspondent. Four brave strangers.
Will they live to keep a promise?

Dan Armitage leaves his job as a war correspondent and meets four people battling for life with two weapons. Hope and humour. Defiant against a deadly disease, the wise-cracking group soon become friends.

As the bond deepens, the five promise to fulfil a wish if they're still alive, but light-hearted shifts to sinister, when Dan's snooping draws him into a criminal web, and he's held captive by a murderous gang.

Can Dan's new friends save him? Will they live to meet again? Find out in this soft-boiled story as laughter and love collide with crooked crime.

If you like pages bursting with remarkable characters, bags of gags, and a splash of sweet romance, then you'll love Frank Malley's absorbing cosy mystery.

Available from Amazon in paperback or Kindle format.

ALSO BY WHISPER PUBLISHING

Released worldwide on 10 November 2021

Two mysteries to solve. Who can Keira trust?

Keira Brody's Roman holiday isn't living up to the hype until mysterious compatriot Leo Callinan walks through her door. Journalist Keira smells a big story.

Enigmatic Leo is charming and fun, but why the secrecy about his trouble with the local authorities and why is one particular policeman hostile towards him?

Determined, Keira vows to help Leo. Will the decision make her career or break her heart?

Available from Amazon in paperback or Kindle format.

ALSO BY WHISPER PUBLISHING

Released worldwide on 10 September 2021

What happens when fortune makes a shy bachelor eligible?

Harold Pettigrew leads a sheltered life. Nearing 40, he's never had a girlfriend, rarely left his hometown, and a strict father and possessive mother have kept him in line. Harold's job at the public library is his only escape. Then things change.

A vast lottery win finds Harold on a luxury cruise with six women as companions, but what are their motives? Do they know of Harold's secret fortune? Does his eligible bachelor status arise from wealth or genuine attraction? Who is not the happy holidaymaker they seem?

Board the Lottery Loveboat and live a warming story of romance, revelation and intrigue, with one petrified millionaire.

Available from Amazon in paperback or Kindle format.

Printed in Great Britain
by Amazon

22986291R00142